Beyond

Light

All fiction
But the rest is true

Michael Remler

First Edition Design Publishing
Sarasota Florida USA

Beyond Light
Copyright ©2024 Michael Remler

ISBN 978-1506-911-82-3 PBK
ISBN 978-1506-911-83-0 EBK

April 2024

Published and Distributed by
First Edition Design Publishing, Inc.
P.O. Box 17646, Sarasota, FL 34276-3217
www.firsteditiondesignpublishing.com

Contents

PART I
THE MURDER

CHAPTER 1

WHY?

"Because of a bullet between the eyes."

Officer Dave could see his captain didn't believe him. Dave did not like having a woman boss who was much younger than him. It had shown in his voice, which was not as strong as he would like. He straightened his back, pulled in his stomach, and then spoke with more authority.

"Actually, that's not it. That was probably the third bullet. He may have been down for a few minutes when that bullet was fired. He was probably really killed by the second bullet to his chest, pretty much straight into the heart. We're guessing. We'll know more after the coroner's autopsy. The first was to the stomach. Then, when he was down, he was finished off with the one to the heart. The last two were just for … for love. First to the head and then to the groin."

"Why to the groin?"

Dave laughed. "Do you really have to ask?"

Mercedes was embarrassed and blushed. Her cheeks started to match her red dress, and her bright red lipstick. "I guess not."

"It's what makes the world go 'round."

That's true. "Who is he?"

"We don't know. There was no ID on him or in the room. The name and the stuff he used to check in the hotel are fake. The credit card is stolen. He was found by housekeeping when they came in to clean. He'd been dead for hours."

Dave had used his military background to help him get this job with the police. He had no special virtues, but he was a hard worker and honest. He was excellent at his job and the brass felt lucky to have him. Nevertheless, they had promoted this much younger woman over him, and it hurt.

Mercedes started to leave. "Call me when you know something. I'll be out for a few hours."

He watched her hips sway as she walked out. *Dammit! She gets away with anything she wants.*

The hotel room was a standard expensive room, with extra chairs, large screen video, etc. Like all hotel rooms, it was fundamentally a lie, intended to make you feel at home by being the opposite of home, because its whole reason for existence is that you are not home. Most specifically, it would have none of the mess and wear of a real home. This hotel room was immaculate even with a dead body in it. The skin around the bullet hole had been cleaned up. In that sense, even the bullet hole was perfect. The bed was still perfectly made. The corpse was neatly dressed. Crisp white shirt with a red tie and no blood stains anywhere. His arms were folded perfectly on his chest. There was not one scrap of litter. The toilet had not been used.

The man at the hotel desk was short, with a mustache. After showing the police badge, "I am Officer David Good. Can we step into an office to talk?"

The desk clerk was visibly nervous in the presence of the police. "Yes sir, of course."

"You were on duty at the desk when he checked in?"

The office was small, with papers scattered everywhere, and the wall covered with official memos. "Yes, sir."

"What can you tell us about him?

The clerk started to clean up the mess, even as he was talking. He seemed to feel the presence of a police officer was akin to an inspection. "I don't know what he looks like now after being shot up, they said four bullets, but he was very handsome. He was tall, over 6 feet. He looked athletic and even agile. A nice face with a very square jaw. He looked at Jennifer, the concierge on at the time, for a few seconds, and I could see she was ready to go to his room with him."

Dave laughed, "Are you kidding me?"

"No sir."

This case could be fun. "Does she do things like that?"

"Not at all. I know one of the managers tried to hit on her several times and she just told him to get lost. She's very proper, but she just kept on staring at him, smiling, and trying to be noticed. It is part of my job to notice such things."

This guy is so nervous it's comical. "This is a picture of him. It's the same man, right?"

"Yes, sir"

"Anything else about him?"

"Oh yeah. He made an impression. He was very clever. He noticed the white, red, and green colors on a little lapel pin I sometimes wear. I was born and raised here but my family is from Bulgaria, and it's a pin my grandfather gave me. He started talking to me about Bulgaria and he knew a lot. He knew things I didn't, especially about the Ottoman period."

"I don't even know where Bulgaria is."

"Most people don't."

"Did you talk to him for long?"

"I did. The desk wasn't busy. My family is originally from what they used to call Adrianople, which was once the Ottoman capital. He knew Ottoman history very well. You don't meet people like that very often and it does make you light up when people know things you care about."

"Anything else?"

"He had no luggage."

"So?"

"He wasn't traveling. That wasn't why he wanted a hotel room."

"Did anyone go to his room? Correct that. Obviously, the killer went to the room. Did anyone see or otherwise know a person who went to the room?"

"No, and we've checked with all the doormen and others who work in the lobby."

Another officer intruded, "Sir, it's ok to move the body to the morgue?"

"Sure. I'm almost done here."

Dave turned back to the clerk. "Anything else?"

"One other thing. The clothes he has on in your picture of him dead are not the ones he was wearing when he came in."

"And he had no luggage …" *The killer brought a new set of clothes for him and dressed him again after the murder.*

CHAPTER 2

WOMEN

The little girl did not know she was an orphan, and her mother did not know she was a widow. They sat comfortably in the large living room of their lavish home. "Where is Daddy?"

Caroline stared blankly at her daughter. There was nothing she could do about it. "I don't know, sweetheart." Caroline was pretty, but not beautiful. She was small, and delicate, with marvelous cheekbones and blue eyes. Her shoulder-length blonde hair made her look almost like a toy model. Everything about her told the truth. She was good, but not strong. The real problem was that her greatest virtue, her sweetness, had been all but drained out of her.

"When will he be home?"

"I don't know. I sort of thought he'd be home by now."

"He was gone all day yesterday."

"I know. He has to go away some days." *There's nothing I can do about it. I guess I'm adjusted to that, but you can't expect a little girl to understand.*

"Can you call him and find out? I need his help."

"I did and there was no answer." *He might be with some woman. I thought he dumped the last one, but maybe not. Men ...*

Johnny was Dave's assistant. "The ballistics came back."

Dave's office was little more than a cubbyhole, with peeling paint, worn-out furniture, and various notices pasted all over the walls. "Yeah?"

"Looks like from a Ruger LCR. The killer was a woman?"

"It's a woman's gun. I'd bet money on it."

Johnny smiled. He enjoyed the idea that this case would have some sexy jazz to it. "That fits with the bullet to the groin. His wife found out he was cheating and arranged to kill him in a hotel room to deflect attention?"

"Could be. Or maybe it was the girlfriend, and he wanted her one last time before dumping her. But how is it so well planned and the room so neat?"

"What about a post-honey trap? They had used him, perhaps for some foreign government, and were now done with him."

"That's getting too wild. Wait 'till we know more before we go off the deep end."

"I'm Officer Dave Good. You're the manager?" *Very posh office.*

"Yes. I am the general manager in charge of the whole hotel."

She has no flesh, no curves, no smile, no nothing. I don't know which is harder to take - a sexless woman like this or one who has it and flaunts it like Mercedes.

The manager then proceeded to waste almost 20 minutes of Dave's time, telling him how important she was and how big an operation the hotel was.

"When did you learn of the dead body?"

"I logged it at 10:43 AM. I was called by the head of housekeeping immediately after the maid found the body."

"And what did you do?"

"Told them to touch nothing and called you."

"Anything else?"

"Yes. Not recently, but last year a man looking just like him came a few times. One of the doormen recognized him. He always came alone and left alone after midnight or a little later. He did not stay the night. We never saw the women come or go that we know.

"How do you know he met women?"

"I just assumed."

"Reasonable but not useful." *She may not look like much but she knows her business.*

"The old security camera tapes from back then are deleted. They are not kept that long." As Dave was about to leave, "One more thing. We can't find the security camera tapes before, during, and after the time of the murder."

"What did you say?"

"You heard me. We can't find the security camera tapes for the whole time before and after the murder could have been committed."

"How is that possible?"

"I don't know. You are the police."

"It's your hotel. You told me you were in charge of everything."

"I'm in charge of everything, but I don't do everything. There is a nighttime security officer whose job it is to monitor the surveillance cameras. I don't know where he is."

"Find him or else!" If you think about it, it's a little bit pathetic, but the truth is Dave enjoyed flaunting his authority at the pompous woman.

Mercedes was seated in her office. "Do you have anything to report?"

Dave stood as a respectful subordinate should. "Not really. We think he was killed by a woman."

"Why?"

"Ballistics said Ruger LCR."

"It fits nicely in your purse. I used to carry one if I went to a club I didn't trust." Mercedes Hererra was a lady of parts. She was 5'7" tall and always wore 3-inch spikes to be almost as tall as the men or taller. She could come to work dressed to kill, and then be the most ruthless bureaucrat in the building. Hidden behind the façade were fears and dreams. But the combination worked. She was the rising star of the police department.

Dave stared lamely at her. "I don't carry a purse."

Don't be a smart ass with me. "I know."

"Captain, there's nothing to be done now really until we know who he is, so if it's ok with you I'm going home."

"Sure. But you need to produce on this case. The Chief has called me twice already. He rarely calls even once. And wouldn't even say why he was interested."

That's your problem. "I'll do my best. You can take over if you want." It's not like David hadn't handled dozens if not more murders in his career, but he could not stop thinking, *you should drop the case before you start.*

What is it with men? They can't learn to wear a saddle if a woman is sitting in it.

Dave had joined the Navy straight out of high school. He deployed and his wife Carmen stayed home with their baby. She got a job as a legal secretary, and when the lawyer started to spend time and money on her, the affair started. When Dave came home, she managed to keep it a secret. Dave knew in his heart, whatever the problem, as always, it was a woman's fault. He did not like having a woman as a boss.

When Mercedes got home, she just slumped down on the couch. It had been a long day, and she felt she had nothing to look forward to just now. There was an exam next week in her course on modern European history, but she didn't want to study. Her life was a full-time job, taking courses in the hope of going to graduate school, and giving time to support her parents who had done so much for her. She was between boyfriends and had no one to talk to. All she could do was make dinner and go to sleep but not before she got down on her knees to pray as she did every night. *Where is my life going?*

CHAPTER 3

THE BIGGER THEY ARE ...

When Dave arrived at the office the next day, Johnny was waiting. "He died about eight pm."

"That's less than an hour after he checked in."

"The killer knew exactly when he was going to be there. She arranged it."

Dave leaned back in his chair. "He didn't go there to be murdered."

"But she got him there to murder him. His wife found out he was cheating and arranged a romantic evening in the hotel so she wouldn't have to kill him at home."

Dave smiled. Johnny was young enough to be his son, but he liked him. *He's a kid enjoying a sexy story. But there's work to do.* "But why the fraudulent identification? She must have known we would find out who he was and suspect her?"

"Maybe she's stupid?"

Dave, "This murder was meticulously planned. The killer is not stupid."

"She hated him so much she made mistakes."

"I guess it could be, but it doesn't sound right."

"So, it's not a wife or even a live-in girlfriend. A woman who on one hand, had a strong enough connection to him to be sure he would be there when she wanted him but also believed we could not trace him to her."

"Can I speak to my husband?" *It's very humiliating. They must laugh at me every day, knowing how many girlfriends he has. And I have act as if I don't know.*

"I'm sorry, Mrs. Alteman, he did not come in to work today. We were about to call you. Did he tell you he was coming in?"

"No. He did not come home yesterday. I thought he might be away on work." *Not really, but what else can I say?*

"No. Did he tell you we had sent him somewhere?"

"No. I was just guessing."

"I think you need to call the police. Maybe he's badly injured in a hospital."

"I think you're right." *That could be true. Then I should call. But if he's just spending more time with some woman it could get very embarrassing. I don't know.* "Can I please speak to Mr. Rathbone?"

"Of course."

"Solly, do you know where Ted is?"

"No. You don't know either?"

"No, and this is unusual even for him."

"I guess that's true. Are you OK?"

"I don't know. I feel very ill at ease."

"We are trying to check up. Please let me know as soon as possible if you hear. He was working on an extremely important account and there is no one else here who can do what he does like him."

"I will. And similarly, if he comes in ask him to call me immediately."

"For sure. Your voice sounds terrible. Have you been crying?"

"Yes ... well only a little bit. I'm sorry."

"Remember, I'm here for you if you need me. Always."

"I know. Thanks." *Thank God.*

Johnny rushed into Dave's office. "The fingerprints are back. His name is Theodore Alteman, known as Ted. He's an attorney. He once worked for the San Francisco US Attorney's office, so we have a full federal database."

"Does he have a record?"

"Disorderly drunk when he was seventeen. Since then, clean as a whistle. Not even a traffic violation."

"What kind of guy is he? Do we know?"

"Top of the line all the way. Haverford College and Chicago Law School. Four-year letter athlete. Straight to Wall Street and the big money. Walked away to join the US attorney's office as a public service. Walked away because he disagreed on the enforcement of immigration policy. Now in a power firm in San Francisco. Top of the line all the way."

"Where does he live?"

"Tiburon, very rich."

"Married?"

"With two kids, a girl - eight and a boy - ten."

"Anything else?"

"Played pro basketball for two years in Turkey after college. Almost got an offer for the NBA."

Dave looked up with a startle. "That's how I know him. When I was in high school, I was a serious athlete. I was the quarterback of my high school football team but I also played basketball. I went to a couple of those camps where the elite colleges look you over. I didn't last the week, but he was there and he got scholarship offers. I didn't know he went to Turkey."

"I looked up his bio and he was amazingly good at everything he did."

"Did he fly by flapping his arms?"

"No, but his brother is a Marine colonel."

She usually worked almost incessantly, but in that moment Mercedes was daydreaming a bit wistfully about her life. She was rudely interrupted when the phone rang. "Mercedes, this is the chief."

"Yes, sir. What do you want?"

"Do you know who that dead man is?"

"No, has he been identified already?"

"Yes, they just called me direct. He's Ted Alteman."

"I'm sorry, am I supposed to know who that is?"

"Yes, he's a very big fish. You can take my word for it, they'll be down on us like a ton of bricks to break this case. And that means I'll be on your back all the way. Sorry, but that's the way it is."

Mercedes was more than a little shocked at the Chief's tone. The truth is he was usually rather paternal. He was proud of his role in promoting this young Latina star. But this time his voice was almost harsh. He meant to grab her attention, and he did. She called Dave immediately. "The dead man is Ted Alteman. They tell me he's a big-shot lawyer."

"I know. Johnny just told me."

"Go check up on him immediately."

Yes ma'am.

CHAPTER 4

ENEMIES

"The chairman is waiting for you in his office." The secretary showed Dave into a large office. Solomon Rathbone was short, fat, pudgy-faced, semi-bald, and unattractive in almost any way you can think of, but he did have confidence, and the short firm movements of his body made that clear. He walked Dave over to two very comfortable seats, which looked out through a floor-to-ceiling window at a fabulous view of San Francisco. *Rich bastards!*

"I'll tell you frankly, I've been chairman of this law firm now for more than thirty years and this is the most terrible, inexplicable, and depressing event I have ever experienced." The chairman jumped up, waving his arms, putting his face right next to Dave's, and jabbing his finger all over the place.

Get out of my face. "That's quite a statement."

"And maybe an understatement. He was unique. One of the most widely admired and most widely hated men I have ever met."

"You know, from almost the first moment I started on this case, I've had the thought I should quit. Now you say this. It feels weird."

"I am one of the most famous lawyers in this country. He wasn't old enough to displace me, but if he had wanted to, he could have. Lots of lawyers know lots of law. Lots of lawyers can make up some fancy reason why their position in a case is right, and for most cases that's more than enough. But for the special cases, you need to recast the question and that was what he could do. He could take a case he was given, take it apart, and reassemble the parts as a different question altogether. I don't know what we will do now without him."

"How is that?"

"Ted had a very unusual background. He was born in a small town west of Wichita Kansas, where his father was the preacher at an evangelical church. From what I've been told, fire and brimstone were the least of what was produced every Sunday. His mother came from a wealthy Quaker family near Philadelphia. He was by all accounts the smartest kid they had ever seen at his school, but I think it was still his mother's connections that got him the scholarship to Haverford. Even through law school, he was hyper-religious. Always preaching to his classmates. It didn't make him very popular. Then, and I've never really understood this, he went to Turkey to play basketball. I think that's where he began to become less religious and more like a real person. Then, for a few years, he was with a firm on Wall Street, with close connections to the banks, and made big money. That's when the two sides of him emerged. On one hand, he continued to do a lot of charity and other good works, but he also developed a taste for women and fun. He went briefly to the San Francisco US Attorney's office before he came to us. That's how he became a fabulous lawyer, making big money, doing good works, and also having affairs and fun on the side.

"Did he have enemies?"

"Too many to count."

"Really?"

"I'll give them to you in groups, and then if you want, I can give you as many names as I know within each group."

"You must be kidding?"

"Not at all. There are all the lawyers he beat in court. There are all the clients of those lawyers he beat in court for a lot of money.

Also all the women he seduced and dumped. The woman's husbands or boyfriends, etc. And then there are people who he humiliated for no good reason."

Holy shit! Dave was stunned. "You must be kidding. They would kill him?"

"Start with the easy ones. He was very arrogant about his strengths. When he had an intellectual argument with you about anything - law, politics, women, even food … whatever, when he won, as he usually did, he would make you feel stupid, in a way that was as if he was being polite but in fact, he did want to hurt you. He would comment that the key fact by which he won, was one he had learned in grade school and thought even dolts knew that. You could put me in that group."

"You don't kill a man because he won an intellectual argument."

"In my world, being smart is the most important part of many people's identity. I know three men I would say hate him for things like that."

"Enough to kill him?"

"Maybe."

"Who else?"

"There is the head of Super Studio in Hollywood who he beat in court for a cool one billion dollars."

"I remember that case." *Everyone does.*

"Sergei Mikhailovich Gulov."

"Who?"

"The power behind the nominal head of the studio. A Russian oligarch, who when he plays nice could convince you that he's the sweetest guy on earth, but when he plays rough, he's the worst of the worst. He's known to have a lot of friends on this side of the pond, who are also investors, also with rather violent reputations. Two of them, Juan Ramos and 'Cuca' Lopez, are big shots in the drug business."

"What's Lopez's name?"

"Cuca, a nickname for Cucaracha, the cockroach."

"I've heard of them. But that was a few years back. Even if they wanted to kill him, why did they wait so long?"

"I don't know. Oh, I doubt it was either of the last two. They have short memories. But Gulov never forgets and always wants to get even."

"Anything else?"

"There's always the women, or more likely the husband/boyfriends of the women, but maybe some of the women."

"Like who?"

"There is one of our partners, Tyrone Neal. Ted seduced his wife and kept it secret for a while. When Tyrone found out, he divorced her, and the affair ended. We kept it so very quiet that almost no one knows. Ted and Tyrone had a fistfight in this office right where you are sitting. It was ugly."

"Enough to kill?"

"He says now he's over it, but honestly, I think yes."

"We need to talk to him."

"He's very polished but underneath he's a very tough man. I would not want to cross him."

"Any others in that group?"

"One is the husband of a doctor down at Stanford. I think her name was Sally Moore. I was told her husband found out and was very angry. They said he was a wrestler in college, and I know Ted didn't come in for a few days."

"Any others?"

"Well, he was usually seeing a new woman about every six months, so there must be a few recent enough to be plausible. I don't remember the names, but I'll get you a list. And I wouldn't count out some of the women. Ted's wife is one tough woman and was livid when he found out."

"It sounds like he wanted to get killed or at least he enjoyed the risk."

Yes, revenge of the jilted woman. While Dave was still in the Navy, he and his wife had two more kids, with at least one of whom Dave was almost certainly not the father. In retrospect, it's hard to understand why Dave never noticed that she wore jewelry that was vastly too expensive, and the out-of-town cases were always in nice vacation spots or interesting cities, but he didn't. Even when he left the Navy, she didn't try to hide it and when he took a job as a long-haul truck driver, it was again easy. The end came because Carmen wasn't the lawyer's only girlfriend. Carmen knew that and accepted it as unavoidable, but when the lawyer dropped one, the dumped woman decided to get even and sent Dave a letter. Dave was devastated but even more so when he realized that for years, he had been the butt of many jokes. They were divorced. All that was many years ago, but the pain and humiliation were undiminished.

Women …

CHAPTER 5

CAROLINE

Tyrone's voice, even over the phone, was obviously nervous. "Solly ... Solly, what did you tell them?"

"What could I tell them? They're the police. I can't lie."

Don't play games with me Solly. "So obviously I'm a suspect?"

"I imagine you will be. I've known you a long time Tyrone, so I'm sure you're innocent. But they don't know you. And we both know you have a great motive."

Dripping sarcasm, "Thanks a lot. With friends like that who needs enemies?"

"Come on Tyrone, I am totally loyal to you. But we both know I can't lie to the police."

"Fair enough. But it ... it makes me very uncomfortable. Have you spoken to Caroline?"

"Not yet. But I'm sure I will."

"She is a suspect also."

Solly pictured Caroline in his mind. *Tyrone doesn't know.* "I'm sure that technically she is, but she is so much not that type, I'm sure they'll drop her quickly."

Tyrone's voice was filled with pain. "Once upon a time, I might've said something like that. But now I know any woman is capable of anything. I doubt that she did it, but you never know."

"She put up with so much for so long. Why now?"

"Every day is a new day. She had plenty of reason."

"No matter what they say, I won't believe it."

Solly sounds too smug for my taste.

Johnny rushed into Dave's office. "You won't believe this."

"What won't I believe?"

"All the surveillance cameras, all over the hotel, were turned off from 8 PM until midnight. Exactly the period of the murder."

"You're right, I don't believe it. How is that possible?"

"I don't know, but the guy who is in charge of surveillance there is being brought in now." Johnny walked out.

Something is very weird about this case. He's a big-shot lawyer, with lots of enemies. He is found dead after having come into the hotel with a fake ID. He was promptly killed and left neatly dressed in different clothes than he wore when he came in. The chief and all the politicians want the case solved yesterday. And now the surveillance cameras have been turned off. And if that wasn't bad enough, I'm always getting this haunting feeling that I should drop the case. I don't get it.

Caroline answered the door. "I'm an officer with the San Francisco police department. Can we come in?"

"Yes. It's my husband, isn't it?"

"Can we sit down?"

"Certainly. Over there?"

Caroline pointed to a soft white couch in the living room. The elegance of the room almost took Dave's breath away. There were large, framed pictures on all the walls. There was a huge mirror at one end that almost made the room feel twice its size. There were large French doors opening to a garden.

Shit, just look at all this money. "Mrs. Alteman …"

"You can call me Caroline." *I knew this was going to be different.*

Dave got instantly nervous. *Is she flirting with me?* "Thank you. … I'm Officer Dave Good. When did you last see your husband?"

"Day before yesterday morning, when he left for work? Something happened?"

"Yes ma'am. He's dead."

"Oh my God!" She starts crying.

They sit silently, as at first the sobbing deepens and then lets up and stops.

"Excuse me." She leaves, apparently for the bathroom. *This is the most expensive house I've ever seen. I bet the furniture in this room cost more than I've ever earned. And look at the jewelry she's wearing. Some people are filthy rich.* Caroline returns with the tears wiped away.

"What happened to him?"

"He was murdered."

Oh, God! They will suspect me. What do they know?

"Forgive me ma'am, but why did you guess something happened?"

Think! What should I say? I can't tell them ... "I think if you had met my husband, you would not ask. He was not like other people. If he hadn't been a human being, he would have been a Greek god. He was handsome, smart, athletic, creative, and more. Every single one of my girlfriends told me privately how envious they were. These are happily married women with very impressive husbands. Many of his law partners told me how exceptional he was. And he knew it. The rules for the rest of us did not apply to him."

"Then did you think he might have been arrested?"

"He could be very mysterious. I never really knew most of what he did."

"Do you think he cheated on you?"

"No, but of course. If cheated means he slept with other women behind my back, lying to me. He would never do that. When he proposed, he said flat out that he would have sex with other women, if he felt like it."

Dave's gut twisted. He had been a big man on campus, with plenty of girlfriends. It's a common story. He got Carmen pregnant.

She would not get an abortion or put the child up for adoption. He was too good to desert her, so they were married. With no skills, he joined the Navy. When he was home, she even introduced Dave to the lawyer, and he told Dave how great she was and how he relied on her. This was the excuse for why she had to 'work late' sometimes, and why he needed to take her with him on 'big out-of-town cases.'

"And did he?"

"I have seen women throw themselves at him in front of my face, minutes after meeting him. I'm sure he had plenty of opportunities."

"Do you know who? We think the murderer might have been a woman."

"No. He was a very good husband and father. I was lucky to be his wife. What he did with the rest of his time was his business."

"Weren't you jealous?"

Do you really expect me to answer? Of course I was. "No. I felt sorry for them, because they knew, once they were done doing whatever he wanted with them, he came home to me."

And you expect me to believe that? "Do you know where he went?"

"I didn't track him. I never asked. There were a few times when something came up, like our son got hurt at school, and I wanted to contact him, and I wasn't able to, and I could just feel he was with a woman. But most of the time when he would disappear for a few hours, his phone was off, and he was unreachable."

"Again, did you think he might have been arrested?

"He always felt the rules for others did not apply to him. He was extremely honest, but I always did imagine that other people, envious and maybe dishonest themselves, might accuse him of things just to get some leverage."

"Do you have anything that can help us?"

"I don't think so."

"As we investigate, we will be looking into his life in very great and intrusive detail. That means we will also learn a lot about you. I don't mean to be personal, but do you have anything to hide? Anything we are likely to learn about you that you want to be kept private?"

"Excuse me for a minute." Caroline walked away to her bedroom and looked in the mirror to compose herself. *I need to watch what I do. What can I do? I don't even know where his money is.*

Dave started to walk around the room. *You could almost feel sorry for her. She may be a rich bitch, but she's all alone. I can see how Ted collected enemies. He was a coldhearted bastard. Maybe she did kill him.*

Eventually Caroline came back. "My husband always distinguished between privacy and anonymity. Privacy is you have no right to know what we do amongst ourselves in our own space. We believed strongly in our right to privacy. On the other hand, we felt we had no right to anonymity, to be unidentifiable when in others' lives or spaces. I have nothing to hide. But although we have no right to anonymity, I believe my husband did many things anonymously, or under a false identity. I never did that, but I'm sure he did often." *For all, I know he has three other wives scattered around the country or the world. God help me!*

"Why?" *She looks nervous.*

"Not one of the many women I am sure he slept with and then dumped tried to get even by contacting me. If I was them, I would have wanted to. So, I assume they didn't know who I was. He was either anonymous to them or gave a false identity."

"Did you have a boyfriend? Just to get even?"

"No. I didn't want to get even." *I've got to talk to Solly. I don't believe that.*

Thursday evenings were Dave's regular league basketball game. Even though he was by five years the oldest guy on the team, he was the most athletically talented and in great shape, but not tonight. He missed open shots, threw passes away, and made countless errors. His teammates were not pleased.

"Dave, what happened? Are you sick?

"No. I don't know."

"We are on our way to the playoffs. We need you."

"I'm sorry."

"Are you depressed?"

"No. but since I've been on my current case, I just don't feel right."

"Who gives a shit about your job. Winning the league is all that matters. Drop the case."

Mercedes stood in front of her mirror. *I don't like thongs, they're not comfortable, but there's no choice under those pants. And the pants are hot. They will get plenty of attention. And the new sweater fits very nicely.* She adjusted her hair and put on her heels. She smiled. *Let's do it!*

CHAPTER 6

TYRONE

The partner, Tyrone Neal, was 6' 3" tall, still quite trim with a hard, chiseled face. He came from a hardscrabble farm in East Tennessee, thirty miles east of Knoxville. They were an old Scots-Irish family that had fought and died for the Union. There had been cousins who left the area to work in the coal mines, one had gone to Pittsburg years ago to work in the steel mills, and even one who had gone to the University of Tennessee to play football, but when his parents were called into the high school and told he was so smart they wanted him to apply to Ivy League schools for a scholarship, they were disbelieving and not sure it was a good idea. Only after their minister intervened and told them it was the right thing to do, did they agree. He arrived at Princeton like an immigrant from a foreign country, dazzled and confused, but he left with honors in history. His senior thesis had been on the motivation of Union soldiers from the northern Appalachian Mountains including his ancestors. Even after law school, and even after moving to San Francisco and becoming a partner in the firm, like so many immigrants, he went back to the 'old country' to find a wife. They were tough people and Tyrone was proud of his roots.

Tyrone's office was just as lavish as the chairman's including the floor-to-ceiling windows. Dave just gasped.

"As you know we are investigating ..." Tyrone was fidgeting with his hair and his pen even before Dave got his first words out. He was very neatly and professionally dressed but very anxious.

"Yes. I wish I had done it, but I didn't."

"We were told ..."

"She was a good woman until he messed with her. I could have gotten past the fling. I could have gotten past it going on a bit even after I knew. But then she started to flaunt it at me. She was in love with him and started to make all these little comments about how he was better than me; better looking, more athletic, and on and on. That I couldn't take. If she weren't the mother of my children, I would have loved to kill her."

He's sweating. "He was killed the night before last. Where were you?"

"I own a cabin, well really more of a nice house, in the mountains near Yosemite. I go there to go fishing."

"Did anyone see you?"

Tyrone's voice was angry. "I know you have to do it, but I don't like being interrogated."

"You're right. We do have to do it. Did anyone see you?"

Now pleading, "I still don't like it."

Look at him. He's a rich lawyer, a tough guy, and so nervous. It's pathetic. He's guilty as hell. "As you said, we have to do it. So please just tell me, did you see anyone?"

"There's a café I like on the way. They know me and I stopped there."

"During the night when he was killed?"

"No. I was alone."

"Do you have a new wife or girlfriend?"

"Girlfriend."

"Does she live with you?"

"Yes."

"Was she with you?"

"No. She doesn't like to fish."

"And you didn't get a chance to fish?"

"Susie, my secretary, called me and told me what happened. I knew I would be a suspect, so I came right back."

"So, you have no alibi?"

"You can look at the records of my phone to know where I was."

"You could have left the phone there to cover your tracks."

"Do you want to arrest me?"

"No, but you are a suspect. You had a motive, an opportunity, and no alibi."

"Look, I was a happy man with a great family, great job, and everything going my way until that son-of-a-bitch ruined it for no reason. I'm glad he's dead. I hope he suffered. But I didn't do it."

"All the murderers say they didn't do it." Dave walked out.

Mercedes called Dave into her office. "I need this case solved. I've never seen the chief like this."

"Maybe you put someone else on it."

"No. You're my senior guy in homicide and I need results." *They keep telling me, that I should be understanding that it's hard for an older white man to take orders from a young Latina. I try but I'm tired of his bellyaching.*

Flaunting her power. "I spoke to the dead man's widow, the senior law partner, and the partner whose wife he seduced. I haven't a clue who killed him."

"Then do your job!"

"Ma'am, what do you want me to do?"

"Don't call me ma'am."

I can think of other words to use given the way you look, but we'll skip that for now. This was one of the days when Mercedes was dressed to flaunt her body. "What should I call you, Mercedes?"

"No. Captain will do."

"Captain … captain, since I've been on this case my life is going to hell. I don't know why but it is. It would be better all-around if you replace me. I'll make up for it by doing extra work without overtime."

First, he plays tough guy, and then he whimpers. Mercedes stared at him. "You do want out?"

"Yes captain, please."

He's not a bad guy and he is good at the job. She smiled, "Not now but I'll think about it. What about the widow?"

"She's a rich bitch."

"I'd be grateful if you didn't refer to women in front of me as bitches."

"All right, she's a very wealthy lady, with no obvious purpose or meaning to her life."

"Do you think she committed the murder?"

"She admitted that she had plenty of cause. Everyone knows he had lots of women. But you can also feel sorry for her. By all accounts, the dead man was not very nice."

"Was he cruel enough for his wife to want to kill him?"

"Yes, though she denies it."

"While you're still on this case there is one more thing. I have a report on his bank accounts, and it is very interesting. More than a hundred thousand dollars passed through his accounts some months ago. He had about ten accounts. Almost none of it was reported on his taxes. And so far, almost none of it is traceable as to where it came from or where it went to."

"And what am I supposed to do with that?"

"I don't know."

"I saw the house he lived in with his wife. It's a lot more than I can afford. I've seen lavish houses but not that kind of money. But the chairman of the law firm said he won the billion-dollar Hollywood case a few years ago so maybe it comes from that."

CHAPTER 7

MERCEDES

Mercedes' mother was pregnant before her parents left Guatemala. Then, as planned, they waited in Piedras Negras in Mexico on the border, until she felt the first contractions. Then, a friend hid them in the back of his truck, and they crossed the border and drove directly to San Antonio, her mother went to the emergency entrance of the first hospital they saw and delivered almost immediately. Her parents were deported quickly, but as planned, Mercedes stayed with her father's cousin, until on the third try, her parents crossed undetected. They went to stay with cousins in Oakland, California. After her father got a job as a gardener and her mother cleaning houses, she came to live with them. They had three more children and lived the American dream. They went to church every Sunday and thanked God for their blessings.

They brought the hotel night security guy into the interrogation room at the police station. He was sweaty and twitchy, even before he walked in. Just to stress him a little extra, they let him sit there alone for ten minutes. Then Dave walked in and stared at him until he said, finally, "You are the man in charge of the hotel video surveillance system?"

"Yes, sir. My boss is in charge of all security, but I am in charge of the video system."

"And you were in fact running the system, the night of the murder? Is that correct?"

"Yes, sir."

"Then would you kindly explain why there are no recordings between 8 PM and midnight?"

"I can't. It makes no sense."

Look at the little twit. "Don't bullshit me. The easiest thing would be simply to charge you with the murder. So don't be stupid. Tell me what happened."

"I don't remember."

"You are one step closer to being charged with murder. Even if you got off, it would be the end of your life. So take a deep breath, relax, and tell the fucking truth. Otherwise, I'll book you for murder now."

He started to cry. "I knew it was too good to be true." He started crying again even heavier.

They waited until the crying slowed down. "Did they pay you to kill him?"

"No. No. You can't even think of that." His whole body was shaking. "No. She just told me to turn off the surveillance and leave with her for a little while and after she would pay me."

" What did you do?"

"She was a hooker."

"And then she paid you, and you did not pay her?"

"Yeah."

Dave smiled. "I gotta admit, that's a pretty good deal."

"And she was damn good."

"So, she was with you the whole time."

"Yes."

"So if you're not lying, then she didn't commit the murder either."

"I swear to God, sir."

Do me a favor and don't wet your pants. "And where is the money she paid you?"

"I still have it at home. I can bring it in if you want."

"Yes, we want."

He started crying again.

"What do we know about the partner's wife?

"She lives in the Berkeley hills with her kids and her boyfriend. The boyfriend is a graduate student in art history. She's thirty-eight and her boyfriend is twenty-four. She's some kind of hospital administrator with Kaiser and makes good money. She gets child support but no alimony from her partner. She also sees other men besides the live-in and may have still been seeing the dead man."

Mercedes smiled. "I like that woman. Check her out."

Caroline answered the phone.

"Hi, it's Solly. I thought it would be more discrete to call than to come by."

"I think you're right. Do they suspect you?" *Thank God for Solly.*

"No. And I don't think they will. If wishes were criminal, I would be already in prison. But they are not, and I am innocent."

"Good. I don't want anything to happen to you."

Caroline started to choke up but then regained control. *Except for Solly, I'm alone.* "There is no reason anything should happen to me. I guess they would suspect me if they knew my life, but they don't. Solly, I'm going to need help."

"I could say exactly the same thing."

"Solly, I need you."

"Under no circumstances admit anything between us, and I will do the same. We need to just be discreet until the case is resolved."

"That's right."

When Mercedes was about twelve, one of her jobs was to deliver the rent check to the landlord who lived not far from the apartment they rented. He was a professor, who although he was quite wealthy, owning about a dozen rental properties, lived very modestly. He was from India, Bengal to be exact, but she could not know that. For a long time, she did not even know his name, Krishna Das, although it was on the checks she delivered. The first thing she noticed was that his skin was much darker than hers. His wife had died young, and his only child, a daughter, worked for the World Health Organization in Geneva. He was more than a little lonely and enjoyed the visits by the little girl. At first, her parents were concerned that he might be predatory. He did not have any known girlfriends, but in time it became clear he was just a nice man. After church, she would come by and help him in the garden, and they would talk. To her, he seemed to know everything. He showed her the world of the mind. He became her advisor about all of life; boyfriends, work, money, everything. Years later, when he developed a slow but debilitating illness, she would pray to God to transfer the illness to her, but of course, her prayers were not answered.

When I'm with my parents, it is as if we were still in Guatemala. At work, I have to be tough like the boys. I'd like to be more like Krishna, and think deeply about the world. And I'm a woman, who likes men and fun. I don't know how to make it all work. I don't know what to do next. I don't know the answers.

CHAPTER 8

LINDA

Linda, the ex-Mrs. Neal, showed Dave into the Living room. They sat down. "Why are you staring at me?"

"I'm sorry Mrs. … Mrs. …"

"I still use Neal … Mrs. Neal."

"I'm sorry Mrs. Neal."

"Now answer me. Why were you staring?"

"I think you know you are very beautiful. I apologize."

"I do. That's why I don't like talking to teenage boys and adult men who act like teenagers. I don't need or want compliments. Just business."

"Understood." *Look at the ceiling or the floor or the wall, but it's goddamn hard not to look at her…*

"I had an affair with him. It was over some time ago. I didn't kill him."

"Do you have an alibi?'

"No. I was home alone."

"You have a boyfriend?"

"I'm too old for boyfriends. I have a live-in lover."

"Was he here with you that night?"

Why do I have to put up with this? "No. He went to visit a friend."

"Who? Where?"

"He's an artist and a student with no real income. I let him live here because he's good in bed and fun to be with, but we have separate bedrooms and separate lives."

That guy got lucky. "Did your current lover kill your former lover as a gift to you?"

"Don't be silly. And I didn't want him dead."

"Really? I'm told he dumped you."

"Ted is nothing to me, dead or alive. If my ex would take me back, I would come crawling on my knees and beg. The divorce was all my fault. I have no excuse. He tried to forgive me. He tried to just get past it, and I humiliated him. I treated him like shit until he couldn't take it anymore."

"Why?"

Linda got up and walked over to the wall and faced away. "I don't know. When I look back on it now, it feels alien... She started whimpering. "I'm not sure it was me. I don't remember why I did what I did. I know I did it, but why?"

"I'm sorry for disturbing you."

"It's obviously not your fault. Mea culpa. Mea culpa. Maxima mea culpa."

"So why didn't you kill the man who seduced you, dumped you, and ruined your life."

"That's not what happened. He was handsome but never warm. He was unbelievably sexy but never loving. He was brilliant but never interested in me. I can remember being sexually obsessed with him but never even liking him. And now all the rest is a fog. He didn't seduce me. I threw myself at him and he didn't duck until he told me to get lost."

"Are you serious?"

"I'm not the only woman he had an affair with. Even I know a few after me."

"Can you name names?"

"Off the top of my head, there was Jenny Moore, even during my time. Then there was Sally Harris who was the main focus right after me. And I can give you more."

"Who was Jenny?"

"Jenny is a doctor down at Stanford. I think she's an ophthalmologist. She's tall, blonde, and about five years younger than me. Like me, she was married. But I guess she handled it better than me because after they split, she was still married to the same man. I guess that doesn't make her a very good suspect. I'm not even sure he dumped her and that it wasn't vice versa."

"I'll check her out. And what about the other one, Sally?"

"I'm not sure how good a suspect Sally is either. I think they were still going strong when he was murdered. Sally is a bit of a cowgirl. She has a ranch north of Woodland."

"We'll check her out also. Do you have any other good suspects to mention?"

"Well, I wouldn't rule out his wife. She comes over as meek and weak, but I think she harbors a deep hurt. I think you should consider Jenny's husband. I believe he's a contractor and something of a tough guy. I don't think he would take kindly to someone messing with his wife."

"What about Sally's husband?"

"She doesn't have one. She's quite a player herself."

"It sounds to me like you've been keeping careful track of his life like you're still in love with him. I think you are our best suspect."

I already told you I'm not in love with him. Why do you have to make me remember all the stupid things I've done? Linda stood up, her face flush with anger. "Get out of my house and get out now. You saw my heart bleed and you poured salt. Get out."

"I'm sorry. I didn't mean to offend you."

"Get out! But I have one piece of advice for you as you go. Drop the case. Everyone who has any contact with Ted lives to regret it. Now, get out!"

"You must understand that you are a serious suspect. This flash of anger makes you an even better suspect."

"I don't give a good Goddamn what you think. Just get out of my house now."

George walked in, "What's the problem?"

Linda smiled. "It's under control." Turning to Dave, "This is George Wilson, my live-in lover I mentioned. Meet the San Francisco police officer investigating Ted's murder."

He's almost young enough to be her son.

George walked over and put his arm around Linda. "It sounds, Mr. San Francisco police officer, like you're not welcome."

Linda pulled away and smiled. "I'll take care of it. Thanks."

"I was just leaving."

"Be quick about it."

Dave went to Mr. Moore's office. He was at first reluctant even to speak to him, but after some standard police pressure, he agreed. "I don't want to step on any sensitive issues, but I need to ask you about the issue of your wife and Mr. Ted Alteman."

"I read about that. The son of a bitch deserved whatever he got."

"Did you do it?"

"No. Is that enough?"

"No. Did you pay someone to do it or otherwise arrange for it to happen?"

"No, I dealt with him myself. I went to see him, we got into a fight, and although he fought better than I expected, I beat the shit out of him. And if it makes me a suspect, then I'll tell you that I told him, if he ever touched my wife again, I would kill him, personally with my bare hands."

" It does make you a suspect. I would say a prime suspect."

"Think whatever the hell you want. I also told my wife, that if she ever touched him again, I would kill her also."

"Is she in danger?"

"No. She apologized, and we get along very well now. I think you could say she was flattered that I felt so strongly."

"I need to speak to Captain Mercedes Herrera."
"Speaking."
"I knew the dead man that was in the papers for many years."
"Who are you?"
"My name is Nancy Thompson. I live in San Francisco."
"How did you know him?"
"It's a long story. I first met him when I was 16 years old. I have no idea why he spoke to me. I was dressed like a tramp because I was a tramp, but he never came on to me. Instead, he started to ask about my life. I gave him the usual bullshit that I gave lots of people, but he was different. Instead of trying to bed me, he told me I needed to get an education, and that he would help me, and he did."

"He just met you on the street and in exchange for nothing, began to help you? Is that what you're saying?"

"Exactly. It may be hard to believe but it's true. Needless to say, at first, I didn't believe him. I was sure he was going to try to use me. But he never did. He got me an apartment and supported me for about six years. He would come and check up on me every few weeks or so. And all that time I never knew his name and he never laid a hand on me. If there are saints on this earth, he was one. I believe in God, and I know in my heart He sent him to save me. I owe him my life."

"What do you do now?"

"I am married to a good man. I have a good job as a secretary and a wonderful new baby."

Mercedes was silent for a long moment. "That does sound almost like a saint. Did he preach to you?"

"No. After I realized that he wasn't trying to get me to bed or use me in some other way, I expected that he would try to get me into church. But he never did. And he never preached. And he never told me anything about himself. So to this day, I can't understand how and why he did it."

Basketball the next Thursday was even worse.

"What the fuck were you doing out there Dave?"

"Are you sick?"

They wouldn't stop. "I'm sorry. Everyone's entitled to a bad night."

"That wasn't a bad night. You stunk up the whole place!"

"If you don't want to play, don't."

"Give me a break. I love the game and I love playing with you guys."

Looking straight in Dave's eyes, "I've played with you for almost ten years. On your worst nights, you were better than anyone else. We rely on you. You made us look like shit tonight. That is unforgivable. If your mother died, you should not have played. If you were out all night with some bitch, you should not have played. I don't like looking like shit!"

"I'm sorry." And still, they would not stop.

CHAPTER 9

GULOV

Mercedes could see that Dave was not doing well. So when the chief called her again, for the umpteenth time, on why she had not solved the Ted Alteman murder case yet, she decided to do this part of the investigation herself, but she took a young officer with her just for a little extra security. A trip to New York to see a Russian oligarch would be interesting, so why not?

"Mr. Gulov has been waiting for you in his study."

"We're not late?"

"No, it's his favorite room in the house. He would have been there anyway."

The study was a beautiful, dark mahogany paneled room with bookcases everywhere. There were two comfortable chairs and a couch. Gulov stood up from behind the desk and greeted them with a big smile. He was dressed in pajamas with a bathrobe. Even like that, it was easy to see that he had once been a very successful weightlifter. The muscles just bulged everywhere. Mercedes was wearing a low-cut blouse and a short skirt. She had found that if the men were focused on her body, they could not keep track of which lies they were telling. The music in the background was the Mozart aria, Dove sono. The sensation was ethereal.

"Captain, please have a seat. Make yourselves comfortable. Can we get you something to drink or even a snack if you wish?"

"No, that's very kind of you. I don't believe I will take much of your time."

"You've come a long way from San Francisco."

"We're lucky you happen to be in New York and not Moscow."

"That's true."

"You know why we are here."

"Absolutely. He was an amazing man." Gulov turns off the music.

"As I understand it, you are a major investor in Super Studio and he got a one-billion-dollar judgment against them."

"That's true."

"That must have cost you a lot of money."

"We didn't enjoy it, but that's business."

"Did you kill him or have him killed?"

"Are you accusing me?"

"No. We have no basis to accuse you but you, and the other investors, people you know, have a motive."

"So, you are accusing me." Gulov leaned back in his chair and laughed. "Don't be shy. I'm a big boy. I can take it. Do you think I did it myself, or do you think I paid for it? We both know I have money."

"Paid for it."

"But you have no evidence. Did you think that coming here I would simply confess?

He thinks of himself as a tough guy and me as an idiot. "Obviously not."

"And since I'm not the kind of riff-raff you can pull in and intimidate, you just wanted to see what I would say, hoping for a mistake or a lead by accident."

The short skirt is not working to get him distracted. "You can say that."

"I'm sorry to disappoint you. But let me try to make this long trip worthwhile and teach you something you need to know. This will take a little while. Are you sure you don't want something to drink?"

"No."

"Let's assume for the moment, that on your way out, the butler who let in, told you he had heard me on the phone ordering the murder. You would of course be inclined to believe him. That's why you came. But then I deny it. He tells you he has no evidence except what he heard. You subpoena my bank records and phone log and find nothing. Let me assure you, that if I had paid for the murder, I would not leave such an obvious trail. I did not make my money being either a crude thug or a fool. In short, I think you should give up now, and not waste your time and effort on this case. You have no facts."

"He is too important for us to drop the case."

"I see. Given you can't solve the case you need a scapegoat. There must be some poor slob you can pick up, threaten, frame, and then go home and rest. I'm not the kind of man you need."

"I don't beat up poor slobs, and I don't frame innocent people."

"Forgive me. I'm a Russian, a foreigner in this country. I know in my country we do it all the time. And I know they do it in many other countries, but the United States is more virtuous than the rest."

"There is no need to be sarcastic. We have flaws also. I was speaking only for myself."

"Fair enough, but I think you Americans have a deeper flaw that we don't have. You are proud of this pseudo-naïve optimistic positivism, that there is a right way to work everything out. You have none of the old religious understanding that this world is a vale of tears. You have none of the old sense of realpolitik, that not all conflicts between nations or people can be solved. You have none of the emotional depth to understand that when you have he-said-she-said there is no clear truth one way or the other. Ambiguity and unknowability are the inner truths of life. In a few hundred years, even Americans can learn that."

Clever bastard! "I think you are admitting that you did have him killed but baiting me that you are so much cleverer than me that you can get away with it."

"Think whatever you want."

"Anything else?"

"Let me teach you something. Power is the ability to make people do things that they don't want to do. It comes in many forms. In the course of my life, I have beaten the shit out of a few dozen men, after which they decided of their own free will to do what I suggested. There were other situations, where I offered them money, and they did what I wanted. Some people called that money, a salary. Other people called it a bribe. Sometimes you do them the kindness of warning them that if they don't do what you want, something bad might happen. And there are other ways to make people see things your way. Some people never get the message that they should've gotten. Maybe someone sent Ted a message when he was focused on something else."

"Did you send him a message that he should've paid attention to?"

"No, Ted and I were on good terms."

"What about your friends?"

"You don't deserve any help but I will tell you one thing you probably don't know. I believe he knew the queen."

"What does that mean?"

"If you have to ask, I probably should not have told you."

"You did tell me. So now tell me what does that mean?"

"She's a very mysterious person. When I met her, she was beautiful and everything else a man could ask for. But afterward, I knew nothing."

"Who does know her?"

"No one does. I have been with her a dozen times, and I know nothing."

"Where does she live?"

"I don't know. When she wants to see you she has you picked up and driven to a mysterious location and similarly returned. She even had me flown twice. I have seen her when I was in Europe, America, and Brazil."

"Where is she from?"

"I don't know. She does not speak Russian. I don't hear any accent outside of Middle American English, but I could miss something. Similarly, in French and Spanish. Perhaps she speaks other languages."

"What does she look like?"

"You may not believe this, but I have had sex with her twice, and I don't really know. She's medium tall for a woman, curvaceous, and very animated but she changes the appearance of her face each time so I don't think I could identify her."

"Anything else."

"Obviously she has a lot of money. She is extremely smart and very very tough. When I was in bed with her, I was doing what she wanted every second. And she did it with a mixture of force and coquettishness the likes of which you cannot imagine. No one else gives me any orders but I do exactly what she tells me. It's amazing."

"How do I get to interview this queen?"

"You don't unless she wants you. Let me tell you, Captain Mercedes, you're in over your head. You seem like a nice girl. And I imagine you're a good police officer. But matters of the queen are at a completely different level. Your questions show you're not at that level. If you continue, you're likely to get hurt. And that may be the best for you. If you make the queen angry she can be very vengeful. My guess is that Ted made her angry."

"You are a clever man. I think you may well be guilty, and just trying to put us off the scent. I'll leave now, but you are a suspect."
If he wasn't a Russian crook, he could be a very interesting man.

CHAPTER 10

DAVE

Dave was in Mercedes' office when Johnny burst in. "We found the hooker."

Mercedes, "Who did you find?"

"The woman who got the surveillance cameras turned off. It wasn't easy. We drove around with him to look at all the hookers on the street and he said no. To make a long story short, we found her working another hotel."

"And?"

"And she knows nothing. All she knows is that she got a call, offering her a job. The money for him, the money for her, and the instructions on what to do were in an envelope left at her apartment. She has no idea who made the call or who left the envelope."

Dave, with the most sarcastic voice he could muster, "You want us to believe that?"

"That's what she says."

"So, you find a hooker on the street who gives you a cock-and-bull story, and you believe it, and you bring it to us as the facts. Are you a police officer or a fool?"

"I'm sorry, sir. What do you want me to do?"

"Do your fucking job and get the truth out of her."

Mercedes, "Where does that leave us?"

Johnny, "It leaves us nowhere. We looked at the money that she gave him, and the money that was for her in the envelope. They're all ordinary bills. Absolutely nothing traceable."

Mercedes, "It's a dead lead?"

"It's a dead lead."

Dave, "Let me look into it. There's got to be some way to squeeze more out of them."

After his divorce, Dave started drinking heavily, lost his job, and ended up living on the street. Then, delusional, and hallucinating from drugs and alcohol, he walked out into a street and was hit by a car. It was the best thing that ever happened to him. He spent six months in rehabilitation, and he met his second wife, Maria. She was a nurse. In the hospital, she helped rebuild his body to the point you could see no damage. She was never married, ten years older than Dave. So, when he was discharged, she took him home with her and rebuilt his self-image as a man. She was a devout Pentecostal and took him to church every Sunday and rebuilt his soul. Dave prayed with total sincerity to thank Christ for the salvation He had given him through her.

It is no fun being married to a not very pretty, old lady who's always a little bit preachy, but it's better than being dead. I owe her my life. I went from being a man to being dirt, and she brought me back to life. I owe her my life. I admit, when Mercedes starts moving her ass, I want to reach out and grab it, but I won't. I owe Maria my life.

"The chairman is waiting for you in his office." Just as before, the secretary showed Dave into a large office.

"I'm sorry to bother you again but this case is very strange. I have made no progress. But we received an anonymous call that you had a relationship with the dead man's wife."

"That's ridiculous."

"After we received the call we did some checking. There were almost six months last year when you called her or she called you almost every day."

"What are you implying?"

"Did you have an affair with her? I recommend you don't lie because we will find out."

"No. I did not have an affair with her. I was not romantic with her. I did not touch her except in the most socially appropriate, almost formal, way."

"We have evidence that you visited her more than a half dozen times in that period."

"She's 30 years younger than me."

Dave practically sneered at him. "That's not very convincing. Most men like to hit up on young women."

The chairman leaned back a was silent for almost a minute. "She called very tearfully, saying that he had been neglecting her, away frequently and for extended periods. She thought we were making him do it. I told her we were not, and that was the truth. We were worried about that also. She was very depressed and pathetic, and I felt I had an obligation to make sure she was ok. She begged for help, and I could not say no. That's all there is."

"Don't lie."

"I don't lie. After a few weeks, she started to improve. I did a public service, and I am proud of it. I do like her. She's a very nice lady. Investigate me as much as you want."

"You're a suspect with no alibi."

Mercedes first met the general at the mayor's inaugural ball. At the time, he was still in the service, but a few months later he had retired and was now the CEO of a company. He was almost 20 years older than her, but still handsome, very virile, and now quite rich. He called her the following week at her office, saying that he was just in the neighborhood, and that could they meet for coffee and they did. A week later he called her to ask her to dinner and a Broadway-style show. She had a wonderful time but was a little put off by how insistent he was that he was right about everything. Nevertheless, she was eager to accept his invitation to go dancing. That also was wonderful, until they left, and he insisted that she come to his apartment for a drink. When he continued to ignore her wishes to go home, she drew her pistol from her pocketbook, pointed it at him, and said "Stop the car. I'm getting out." He never called again, but there were a few times when she thought she was being stalked.

Dave said, "I think it's the cowgirl, Sally Harris. We checked her phone logs and she called the dead man two or three times on the day he was killed. That can't be a coincidence."

Mercedes said, "Have you spoken to her?"

"No, but we can go today."

"Absolutely."

Dave went back to the widow.

"I should have told you, but … you may not believe me … but I had almost forgotten the whole episode. It felt like a fog. I know it was me, but it is also alien. I'm not sure it was me."

"Was there an affair?"

"No. Not at all. Ted was away a lot and I felt sad, lonely, and sorry for myself. Maybe deep inside me, I did want an affair, but nothing happened. Almost suddenly, Ted was back with all his charm. When he turned it on, my knees would go weak. That's why I essentially forgot the whole thing when you were here the first time."

"The records we have show that you and Mr. Rathbone were together many times. Not just once. Please don't lie. In the end, we find out, and then it's worse for you."

"I'm sorry. I guess I am embarrassed. Mr. Rathbone did support me many times when I was not feeling well. But I never had an affair with him."

"What kind of a relationship did you have with him?"

"He was more than a friend. I leaned on him a great deal. I imagine I will be leaning on him even more now. But if you're asking did we have sex, the answer is no."

"It's clear that you were not happy with your late husband. And therefore, it is clear that you had a motive to murder him. It is clear that you had a strong relationship with Mr. Rathbone, whether or not it included sex. It is clear that Mr. Rathbone had a motive to murder Mr. Alteman."

On the way home. Dave pulled forward after the light turned green and was hit flat on by a drunk. His police car rolled over. Luckily, he was strapped in and the roof held, so that even though he was badly bruised, there was no serious damage. He was taken to the hospital Emergency Department but released after a few hours. *Thank you Lord for letting me live. He wouldn't do it for me. He did it for Maria.*

Two days after the accident, when he was already pretty well recovered, Dave went to see Mercedes. "Captain, you can fire me, but I am off this case as of now!"

Mercedes looked up and smiled. "I heard about your accident. It's terrible but at least you were lucky."

"Captain, you can fire me, but I am off this case as of now!"

"Why?"

"There is something very spooky about this. His widow and the partner's wife he seduced both warned me to drop it."

"So what?"

"When I asked the partner's ex-wife why she had the affair, not only she couldn't remember but she said it felt alien. When I asked the widow about her flirtation with the head of the law firm, she said it felt alien. They both used the exact same phrase. They don't remember, they were in a fog, and it all seems alien."

"I can't let you go now. I know it's not easy for you to have me as a boss. Believe me, I try my best to be reasonable. Everyone tells me how hard it is for an older man to have a younger woman as a boss. I can't let you go. I just can't."

"Your only choice is to accept my resignation from this case or fire me." He turned and left.

CHAPTER 11

FRANK

Since Dave had dropped the case firmly in Mercedes' lap, she was now stuck with it. There were plenty of suspects: Caroline Alteman, the victim's wife; Tyrone Neal, the cuckold partner; Linda, the seduced partner's wife; and Soloman Rathbone, the head of the law firm who saw Caroline too often; Moore the contractor who played tough; and Gulov, the Russian oligarch. All had no alibi. But still, it felt like there were no leads. They all just didn't look like the killer even if they didn't have strong alibis. It was time to use the old rule, 'Follow the money.' In this case, the Money was the huge fortune that passed through his accounts. The best lead for that was the gambler.

After the funeral was over, the police asked each person as they left to please step aside and answer a few questions about how they knew the dead man. More than a few had very extraordinary stories.

"I saw him only once. It was on the street in New York. My ex-husband was beating me up for no reason. I have no idea why the dead man was there, but he stepped in and stopped my husband, who then drove away cursing me out. The man never gave me his name, but he took mine and my phone number. He gave me $500 in cash and told me to go to a motel and stay safe away from my husband which I did. He then sent money to support me for the next six months while I got a divorce and started my new life. I never saw him again and until today I didn't even know his name. I came to the funeral after I recognized his face in the newspaper."

"When was that?"

"A little more than 10 years ago."

Frank Agri's house was just outside Las Vegas surrounded by a high wall and a gate. Mercedes used the phone box to identify herself and the gate opened. When she reached the house a man came out to meet her. "He's waiting for you inside. I'll let you in and if you give me the keys, I will park your car for you."

The house was pure Las Vegas, perfect, extravagant, and totally fake. The front hallway was bigger than some people's apartment. There was a beautiful, curved staircase coming from the second floor. Mercedes felt unsafe the moment she laid eyes on Frank. *He looked so sleazy. He looked so predatory.* She put her hand on her gun just for reassurance.

Frank was the fourth generation in the business. His great-grandfather was the immigrant. He was a violent man, but that was the only way for him at that time. His grandfather only killed a few men, because the rules of a mob were already well-established. By the time by the time his father came along, the money came mostly from gambling, and they could stay away from the drug cartels. They even had money in Hollywood and other legitimate places. So even if Frank had the mind of a thug, he had very little dirt, and no blood on his hands, but he kept the honest vulgarity and crudity … and the swagger.

"I knew Ted for years when he was my friend before he became a greedy pig. I'm not surprised someone killed him. Maybe I'm surprised it wasn't sooner."

"Did you do it?"

"No way. If I wanted it done, I wouldn't do it myself."

"Did you have it done?"

"No, but probably should have. He'd been asking for it for a long time."

"What does that mean?"

"What do you know?"

"We know that a lot of money passed through his accounts. We know that a lot of it came from you."

Frank started to pace. "I'm a gambler. He was a gambler. We did a lot of business together. When he won, I paid him the money. He was filthy rich, but still, he tried to take advantage of everyone."

"Where did he get the money for all the gambling? And do you know what he did with all the money you sent?"

"In my business, we don't ask questions."

"You have no idea where all of that money came from?"

"He was a big shot lawyer that's all I know. Lately, he went out of his way to piss people off." Frank strutted around the room, jabbing his finger at Mercedes.

Macho and money. Mercedes smiled. "Do you know what he did with the money?"

"I live in the fast lane; money, women, etc. but he seemed to live in a rocket, way overhead, invisible because he was so high up and then dropped in on you and dominated the scene until he disappeared. He had that wife, and kids, and a job, but that was not him. He must have worked for the queen."

Mercedes was surprised to hear about the queen again and did her best to hide it. "The queen? Who's that?"

"You've never heard of the queen?"

Mercedes lied with as straight a face as she could. "No."

"Then drop the case or get someone who does. You're in over your head. The world is divided between those who have experience with the queen and those who don't. You'll never understand anything about Ted if you have never experienced the queen."

"Who is the queen?"

"I'll tell you everything I know, and it will do you no good."

"I'm not stupid. Don't talk to me that way."

"I don't think you're stupid. If I did, you'd be gone already. You're not a bad piece. You have a pretty face and good legs but that's not enough. Why don't you get out of the cop business and work for me? I'll pay you twice or three times what they do."

And make me one of your whores. "No, thanks. Who is the queen?"

"I don't know. Many years ago, when I was young and studly, she summoned me to her, spent the evening with me in bed, and sent me on my way. But the thing about the queen is not only do you not know where or why or anything about how it happened, you almost aren't sure it did happen."

"Are you trying to play me for a fool?"

"No. I know three others who have been with her, and they will tell you the same thing. No one has any memory of what she looked like."

"Now I know you are fooling with me."

"I'm telling you the truth. You came here to investigate Ted's death. I know absolutely nothing. Ask me whatever you want and go."

"Who is the queen?"

"Do you remember what you had for breakfast?

"Of course."

"Do you remember what you had for breakfast this day last year?

"Of course not."

"Did you have breakfast on this day a year ago?"

"Probably."

"But you're not sure."

"I'm not sure."

"But you would have been sure at this time last year."

"Yes."

"Do you know that there are chemicals that block memory?"

"Yes."

"Memory is funny."

"Don't be too cute. You claim that you spent the night making love to a powerful woman who summoned you to her bed out of nowhere and now you have no idea who she is or if it really happened."

"That's it. But with the other fact that I do remember she was known as the queen and I have spoken to others who have had the same kind of experiences. And like me, after they were not sure it happened."

"I still think you're lying to me. Maybe you murdered him and are preparing a psychosis defense."

"That is stupid. I need no defense."

"How do I meet the queen?"

"Only if she wants you."

"Why did she want you?"

"I don't know. The truth is that when I try to remember it, it feels alien. I'm not sure it was about me."

The word alien again. "I ask you again, how do I meet the queen?"

"I have no idea. Since you seem desperate, I will offer you a desperate idea but don't blame me if you get raped or killed. Go talk to El Sueño."

"That's not possible. He's wanted on a mountain of drug and murder charges. They killed a whole battalion of the Mexican Army that tried to reach him."

"So why don't you forget all this, and come and work for me."

"I already told you no." *Mama would cry till the day she died.* "How do I meet the queen?"

"It's easy. Put an ad in a major newspaper asking to meet him. Address it to Pablito Mendoza Garcia. That's his real name, and believe it or not, he will treat calling him Pablito as a secret handshake. Sign it with any name you want, and that will be the code word to go with the people who come for the kidnap. You might have to advertise twice. Then make yourself extremely available to be kidnapped by walking on an empty rural road every night, in the middle of the night. By the third or fourth night, you will be kidnapped and a day or two later, talking to El Sueño. Don't bring weapons or a tracking device. At best it will make you look foolish, and a worst killed before you meet him. It's up to you how you feel if he decides to fuck you, but don't resist. It can only make it worse."

"What does he know?"

"He is closer to the queen than any human being. She protects him. That is how he destroyed that Mexican Army. I don't believe he will explain the murder of Ted or tell you anything, but it is your only hope."

"Stop treating me like a fool."

"You have two choices, stay, have a delicious dinner, and spend the night with me, or leave."

"No thank you."

"One other thing, I advise you to drop the case. Like the Mexican army, people who try to approach the queen about things that they don't want you to know, always live to be sorry."

"I don't get it. One of my officers was also warned to drop the case, and since then, he has refused to be a part of it. Were you told to tell me that?"

"No. Of course not. That's not the way they work. But it is a fact. And whoever convinced your officer did him a favor. I'm just trying to do you the same favor."

Mercedes smiled and left.

CHAPTER 12

SALLY

Sally Harris met Mercedes next to the corral with the horses in it. She wore a cowboy hat and boots, jeans that smelled more than a little bit of horse manure, and a blouse, so tight that if she took a deep breath, she could probably pop two buttons. Even while they were being introduced, Sally seemed more focused on the horses than on Mercedes. "Like I said, I am an officer with the San Francisco police department, investigating the murder of Mr. Theodore Alteman. As we understand it, you know him very well."

"I don't know about very well, but I certainly knew him, and he knew me. I read that he was murdered. It's a pity. He could be a lot of fun."

"As part of the investigation, we have looked into phone logs, and it appears that you called him three times on the day he was murdered. And we didn't see any calls for some weeks before then. Can you explain that?"

"If you're asking me, did I kill him, the answer is no. We had a relationship, but I'm not possessive and I won't let anybody be possessive of me. It occurred to me that day, that since I was planning to go to San Francisco, we could meet and have some fun. That was the first call. The second call was for details, about where we would meet. I suggested the hotel, and he agreed. But later that day, I changed my plans. I called the third time to tell him that I wasn't coming, but he didn't answer. That's all I know."

"Were you setting him up for someone else to kill him?"

"Of course not. I liked him. Why should I want to kill him?"

"He has treated some women rather badly. We have reasons to believe the killer was a woman."

"He had no opportunity to treat me badly. I wanted and expected nothing. I never expect a man to treat a woman well."

"So why did you have a relationship with him if you expected nothing?"

"You're a woman. Are you really asking me that? They're fun but only if you expect nothing. I treated him like a mare treats a stallion that is bothering her. She gives him a little kick. That's what I do, and frankly, I think that's what Ted liked."

"Ted likes being kicked?"

"I didn't mean literally kicking a man. The mares do that to the stallion. Most men are in it only for the ride. If you're in the mood, and they give you a good ride, then why not do it? And if you're not in the mood, then you don't. Ted had a lot of women. Maybe that bothered his wife, but it didn't bother me. So, it was good for Ted, if I wasn't in the mood, to get a nice little kick, and be told to buzz off. As it was better for him to saddle up somewhere else if I wasn't in the mood for him."

" Why did you change your mind and cancel the meeting with him?"

"I don't know. I like to live in the moment, and he did not seem like the right man for that moment."

"You have an alibi?"

"I guess I do. I was with a different man that night. If you have to have it, I can give you his name."

She is a player. "How many men do you have in your harem?"

"At the moment, I guess about four."

"We will need the name of the man you were with."

"He's married."

"Isn't that a problem?"

"It is for him, but not for me."

"Are any of the other men in your harem married?"

"Well, as you know, Ted was, and one other."

"You seem to prefer the married."

"Well with the sexes reversed, that was exactly the advice of Ben Franklin. It makes them much easier to manage."

Mercedes smiled. "You should write a book." *I don't think I could live that way.*

"Maybe I will. Rarely, if they do try to be too demanding, all you have to do is hint at telling their wives, and they snap to attention very nicely."

"We will still need to talk to the man from that night. You need an alibi."

"It's not a problem for me, but does his wife have to know?"

"I'll see what we can do. Did anyone else see the two of you together?"

"No. He came here."

"Maybe he's just lying to protect you, a friend. We may have to ask his wife if she knows where he was that night. Life can be messy."

"I don't need protection."

That's true.

Mercedes asked Dave to see Frank but not before he protested again that he wanted to get out of the case.

"I went to see Frank Agri."

"Really?"

"Yes really."

"He doesn't usually talk to cops."

"I know. They said it was probably because I wear a skirt."

"So?"

"Have you heard of the queen?"

"What kind of question is that? I don't know what you mean."

"There is some mysterious powerful person that they all call the queen. But no one can remember anything about her, even when they say they have met her or spent the night in bed with her."

"Yeah, I've heard of the queen. But do you think it's real? As you say, whenever you ask about it people become very vague. Sometimes I think it's all just street talk."

"Agri may be a murderer and God knows what else, but he's not playing games. We got him scared."

"So?"

"Agri says that if you talk to El Sueño he can tell you anything and everything to do with the queen."

"Give me a break. Now you know that it's bullshit. No one talks to El Sueño. The Mexican army can't talk to El Sueño. And you think he's going to talk to you? You're crazy!"

"Agri says that you can't fight your way in like the Mexican army tried, but if you put yourself at his mercy, then if it interests him, he will talk to you."

"Then go talk to him. What does that have to do with me?"

"I was hoping you would go."

"I told you no. But even if I was inclined personally to change my mind, Maria told you no. I will never go against Maria."

"Well, then at least when you go to see Frank again and see what you can do."

"I'll ask Maria. If she says yes, I'll do it."

"I am the person Captain Mercedes asked you to talk to."

Frank looked nervous. "Come in. I'll talk to you."

"All I want is a little information."

"Information is a big deal. Have you seen El Sueño?"

"Not yet."

"So why are you here?"

"We think you know more than you've told us. There's a lot of pressure on to find the killer. We have orders not just from the chief, but, even from the mayor, to squeeze as hard as we can. Captain Mercedes told me to tell you that we will arrest you on suspicion of murder unless you give us more information."

"I see." Then Frank walked around the room silently for a long time. "I paid for a gun. That's all I know. Maybe that's the clue they want me to give you."

"We need to know, what gun? Where? Who received it? Etc."

"It was a Ruger LCR. I never saw it or touched it. I told them where to put it so that someone else could pick it up. That's all I know."

"Captain Mercedes said that the murder weapon was a Ruger LCR." *At least he's not lying.*

"I guess that's the clue you need. I don't see what good it is."

"Where was it left?"

"I don't remember."

"How did you know where it was supposed to have been left?"

"I don't remember."

"Who put it there?"

"I don't know. I bought it from a guy I know, Harry Gonzales, and I told him where to put it. At least I think I did."

This guy is the biggest sleaze bag I think I've ever seen. "Stop trying to sell this shit! If you keep answering every question with 'I don't know', then the only thing to do is to arrest you. If we keep you locked up, it will improve your memory."

Frank's face turned cold. "Don't threaten me. I helped you more than I should've. Go to hell!"

"No, you'll go to hell. You'll go to the hell they call prison. If I leave like this, we will arrest you as at least an accessory to murder. Stop this crap and tell me what you know. Otherwise, I swear to God, you will be arrested in less than 24 hours."

"Don't threaten me! If you arrest me, I warn you, I have friends. I will give you all the help I can, and if you don't like it, tough shit!"

"Don't you threaten me. Tell me what you've got to say, and then I'll decide if we're going to arrest you." *He's sweating. He's beginning to buckle.*

Again, he walked around the room, not looking at Dave. "I'll tell you everything I know, but believe me you won't understand any of it unless you talk to El Sueño and understand the queen. ... They play with your mind. I don't know if the queen is a real person. I don't know anything. That's why you have to talk to El Sueño. I do know that years ago things happened in my head that scared the shit out of me, but it also made me feel wonderful. And sometimes I get those feelings again. I went to see doctors about it. One thought I might have epilepsy and another thought I might be going crazy. But after all the tests, he found nothing. They even put me on drugs, but they had no effect. When I get those feelings, I sometimes get the feeling I should do something. It's not always clear at all what I am to do or why I am to do it, but I know I must do it and I do. I took some cash out of one of my clubs and sent it to Harry Gonzalez with instructions to buy a gun, distribute the money, and leave a message. That's all I remember."

The rest of the conversation was a waste of time.

Dave reported back to Mercedes.

Mercedes, "Harry Gonzales is a local petty hood. I even think I've arrested him once or twice before I was a captain. What's a big shot like Frank Agri doing using a local piece of nothing like that?"

"Now, you know the money came from Frank. You know how the gun was bought. You also know how the gun was delivered and how the recording system was turned off. It's in your hands now, Mercedes. I've done my part."

"You're not off this case until I tell you. I give the orders. *He's not a bad guy.* "Bring him in and question him. Sweat him some more."

I'm tired of you flaunting your ass and your power.

CHAPTER 13

IF YOU BELIEVE IT

"No! and that's a direct order. No! That is the craziest idea I have ever heard. We will not send a female officer, unprotected into the fortress of a monster criminal, at the suggestion of a shady gambler. Agri's just another suspect without an alibi, but able to sweet talk you into buying a cock-and-bull story."

Even in his 60s, when everyone expected he would retire soon, the chief was a very impressive physical specimen. He was 63, 190 pounds, and still the remarkable athlete he had been as a young man. With Mercedes he could be alternately paternal, and then at times a suggestion predatory. She had never seen him like this before, so flush and demonstrative.

"Chief, there are no other leads. Do you want to give up?"

"Better than getting you raped."

"Do you want me to give up?"

"No. This is a big case. If we fail on this, it will be the only part of my whole career anybody remembers."

"So?"

"Go back to the partner whose wife he seduced. Do something! I don't care what! I want this case moving."

Thanks a lot, boss.

Before she had a chance to do anything, Dave barged into Mercedes' office.

"Captain Mercedes, I want you to meet my wife, Maria."

Mercedes was confused. "What is this about?"

"My husband is off this murder case."

"I'm sorry Mrs. Good, but you do not make policy for the police department. This is a standard investigation, and he's been assigned to do it."

"If you insist, I will tell him to resign."

"Why?"

"Because we have prayed together, and it is the will of the Lord."

"I'm sorry Mrs. Good, but I can't accept that."

"You may do as you wish Captain, but my husband will follow the will of the Lord."

Not without more than a touch of sarcasm, Mercedes asked, "And how do you know the will of the Lord?"

"We pray. And when that is not enough, we pray more. And if we need help, we go to our pastor, and we all pray together. And then we look into our hearts, and ask ourselves, 'What does Jesus want?'"

"And what did Jesus say?"

"We could feel in our hearts that this was a very dirty business. My husband has had a hard life. For many years, before he found Christ, he was involved in the ugly side of life. He has worked hard to reach his salvation. I understand that my husband does police work and that requires associating with dirty stuff. We accept that. We believe that he does that work in the service of the Lord. But this case just feels different."

"Did your husband tell you that the dead man had done some incredibly generous things? At least two people have called us to tell us that anonymously. He virtually saved their lives. Isn't finding his killer doing God's work?"

"Perhaps it might've been, but we have prayed and made a decision."

"Mrs. Good, I also go to church regularly. I also pray every day. I also am grateful for my salvation. But Jesus does not tell me what to do. With respect, I don't understand."

"I am glad to hear that you pray. I don't know what you want me to say. Our Lord reaches each of us in different ways. I can tell you that the Lord does not wish my husband to continue on this case. I beg you to respect that."

Mercedes went to see the chief again. "It's not like we don't have suspects. We have plenty. There's the widow; the partner whose wife he seduced; that wife that he later dumped; the head of the law office who was trying to make time with the widow; the contractor whose wife he had also fooled around with; and more. There are plenty of suspects, but my gut tells me that none of them are the killer. These people are not natural killers, even the contractor who claims he is."

He told her again it was still a crazy idea, but if she could get Tyrone or some man to go at least she was not at risk of being kidnapped herself and raped. She reminded the chief what he had said, that if this case was not solved it would be the only thing that anybody remembered about his record in office. Reluctantly he agreed to the plan but only with Tyrone, not her.

"I have another problem. Dave Good does not want to continue on the case. His wife came and told me that God had decided he should not continue. I argued with her, but she was adamant. But like I said, that's not the weirdest thing. People all talk about forgetting, about feeling that everything was alien and warning us to drop the case. I'm not going to force Dave, and I'm not going to quit, but you have to know that something is not right."

Mercedes followed the Chief's orders and went back to Tyrone. "I have nothing to add."

"You have the best motive."

"Why not Frank Agri? He took Agri's money. That's motive."

"I went to see Agri and we've checked him out as best we can. It seems he was involved, but that he was manipulated. It seems the murder plot was complicated and that Agri was just a part."

"He's a tough guy."

"Have you heard of the queen?"

"The Queen of England?"

"No, someone very mysterious known only as 'the queen.'

"No ... well maybe ... not really, no ... in a sense ... Why do you ask?"

"What do you know?"

"Why do you ask?"

"Agri thinks Ted worked for the queen and that is why he could do the impossible things he did."

"And you believe that?"

"I don't know what to believe."

"The queen is a myth, an urban folk story, like Jack and the Beanstalk."

"Agri was just playing with me?

"Probably, you wear a skirt."

"I don't think so."

"Think what you want."

"Do you think El Sueño is an urban legend?"

"Hell no. From what I've read, he's one of the biggest drug dealers there is."

"Agri thinks the queen arranged for Ted to seduce your wife. Agri says El Sueño is so powerful and so indestructible because the queen protects him."

"So?"

"Perhaps you want to ask El Sueño how Ted seduced your wife."

"I'm done with her. She's a bitch, just another whore. It's over, ancient history."

"I don't think so. I think you still love her."

After a long pause, "What if I do?"

"You are the most likely killer. At this point, I think we could get an indictment. But if you want to prove that you're not the killer, then we need to talk to El Sueño. Agri told me how to reach El Sueño, and frankly, I would like to do it but my boss said it was too dangerous for a woman and I can't go against him. I would like you to go and talk to El Sueño."

"Go online to get me killed?"

Agri says that if you do it in such a way that you are totally at his mercy, he will talk to you and then let you go."

"Why should I believe you?"

"I'm telling the truth. Also, the breakup of your marriage is the most important thing in your life, and this is the only way you'll ever really understand what happened. Thirdly, from what I've read, and speaking to you, you are a very intelligent man and interested in deep things. There is every reason to believe there is a very deep mystery here." *I feel sorry for him.*

Tyrone fell silent and looked off into the distance. He paced. Mercedes just sat there and watched him. He started to speak three times but didn't say anything. Finally, he stared at her for a long time. Then, "What would you want me to do?"

"As I understand it, you advertise yourself to be kidnapped by them and then make yourself available for the kidnapping."

"You want me to ask to be killed."

"Not really. If you put yourself completely at his mercy, and he decides to kidnap you, it can only be that he is willing to talk to you. He has no reason to kill you. You're probably safer under his control, than you are walking the street of any big city."

Tyrone was silent again. "And why do I want to do this?"

"Because if they do agree to talk to you, you will learn things that no one else knows, or could know. And most of all that includes what happened to your wife."

"Let me think about it."

Michael Remler

She threw away a good man. I'd like one like that.

CHAPTER 14

FALLING APART

Mercedes called Dave. "I don't want to get in trouble with your wife, but I need you back on the case."

"No means no. Not maybe. Not sometimes. No means no."

"I'm not really asking you to be back on the case. But I do need a little help on something related to the case. You do realize that this case is very special."

"How could I not? I will remember this case on the day I die. It scared the living shit out of me."

"I think we're on my way to breaking it but I need your help."

"I told you no. I meant no. I'm sticking to no. The answer is no!"

"Dave, we've known each other a long time. At least hear me out."

I hate the way she uses sex, but she really is a good person. "OK, but don't expect me to change my mind. There's something very spooky about this case."

"I want to go see El Sueño, but the chief won't let me. But he said it's OK if a man goes."

"Are you asking me to go?"

"Maybe, but for now, no. I asked the partner Tyrone to go, and he refused, but I think you could talk him into it, man to man."

Mercedes called Dave. "I don't want to get in trouble with your wife, but I need you back on the case."

"No means no. Not maybe. Not sometimes. No means no."

"I'm not asking you to be back on the case. But I do need a little help on something related to the case. You do realize that this case is very special."

"How could I not? I will remember this case on the day I die. It scared the living shit out of me."

"I think we're on our way to breaking it but I need your help."

"I told you no. I meant no. I'm sticking to no. The answer is no!"

"Dave, we've known each other a long time. At least hear me out."

I hate the way she uses sex, but she is a good person. "OK, but don't expect me to change my mind. There's something very spooky about this case."

"I want to go see El Sueño, but the chief won't let me. But he said it's OK if a man goes."

"Are you asking me to go?"

"Maybe, but for now, no. I asked the partner Tyrone to go, and he refused, but I think you could talk him into it, man to man."

Mercedes finished cleaning up after dinner at her parent's house. She went there at least once a week to make them dinner and do other things to help take care of them that they were now too old to do for themselves. To herself, she called it paying the mortgage. After all they had done for her, she owed them. She always said to herself, *Love is cheap, but work is real.* "I've got to go. I have a paper due in two days for my course on English history. I need some ideas, and I'm going to meet Steve, one of the guys in the class, to discuss things. I'll be back in a few days."

They met at a coffeehouse near campus, found a table in the corner, and set up their laptops.

She's pretty, a cop, and takes advanced university courses. I'd love to get my hands on her.

Mercedes, "Who are you going to do?"

Steve was still looking her over. "Oliver Cromwell, I think. He's the most important man in that period."

He could see that she was not pleased with that answer. "And who are you doing?"

Mercedes smiled, "Charles the Second."

"Why him? He wasn't very nice to women."

"On the contrary, he loved women."

"Well maybe for sex, but he didn't treat them as equal, as real people."

"No, you have it completely backward. He was a man who liked fun and liked women, and if it ended in bed, that was OK too. But at the beginning and in the end, he liked women. I don't think you need to use modern feminist ideas to judge a 17th-century king."

"Then how would you judge him?"

"As I judge myself. An honest human being, trying to make their way in life. He had an impossible situation. He believed in the Catholic Church, and his country believed in the Anglican church. To survive he needed to lie, and he did. That's life."

"Then, why don't you prefer Cromwell? For better or for worse, he upheld his convictions."

"As his country made clear, it was for worse. As soon as he died, they went in the opposite direction."

"Maybe so, but do you approve of the direction that he wanted to go in? Do you approve of seeing women primarily for sex?"

"All men do. It's just that he …"

"Look, I like women. I like you. If we ended up in bed, that would be good too. But I have tremendous respect for you. I respect your intelligence to go to graduate school. I respect your toughness as a cop. I respect your goodness as a person to come here after taking care of your parents. And I respect that beautiful body that you like to show off."

Mercedes smiled again, "It's a pretty good pick-up line, I have to admit."

"I hope it works." It did but she was disappointed with the results.

Walking home alone, her mind wandered. *I wish I knew what I wanted. I want good-looking, but that's just a start. And if you can get everything else, it's not that important. Steve is OK at that but nothing special. And not that good as a lover. But he is smart, and nice, and attracted to me. Maybe I should give him another try.*

When Dave knocked on Tyrone's door, he let him in. "Captain Mercedes said you turned down going to see El Sueño. I'm here to change your mind."

"I told her I would think about it. Whatever I decide, you can't change my mind."

"Can I come in?"

Their eyes met. Tyrone let Dave into the living room. "Do you want a beer?"

After a few other minutes of pleasantries, they were relaxed with each other.

"Let me try. This case is like nothing else I've ever seen. I've already refused to be a part of it, and I've been talked back into it. If I can change my mind, you can change yours."

Just leave me alone. "You can't. I don't think you understand. That woman drained all the blood out of my soul. I loved her so much that I could not imagine anything else in the world. When she started to cheat, I wouldn't believe it. When there was no way to avoid the truth, I begged her to stop. She said she would but didn't. When I confronted her again, she just laughed at me. When I begged, and begged, and begged, instead of changing, or even being sympathetic, she just flaunted it. I can't go anywhere near it without crying. The answer is no, and it will stay no."

I don't think I've ever seen a man in so much pain. "I do understand. You are not the first, I was there before you. And the sad truth is, we're not the last. They know they can get away with it, and when they want to, they do. And like with you, they don't care how much pain they inflict."

"That's still not a reason why I should do it."

"There is a real mystery here. It's not how he died, but how he lived. How was he able to destroy your wife? I think that is something you should want to know."

"Yes, but no. I will not do it. I won't relive that pain."

"You know, my wife now is a very devout woman. And she has taught me to give my life to Christ. One of the things she taught me, is that there are things that are in the hands of God and that we simply have to surrender ourselves to Him. I think you should put yourself in the hands of faith, and let it flow."

"I'm glad that works for you, but it doesn't for me. I haven't gone to church since I left home. I don't want to relive the pain, but the truth is, that's not the biggest reason. I would run the risk of leaving my children with her. And as long as I breathe, I will not do that!"

"It's your one chance to understand what happened to her. Why did she destroy your marriage?"

Tyrone paced for a long time, then he said, with tears in his eyes, looking right at Dave, "I have children and I will not take the chance that they fall into the hands of that bitch. No."

The following day Mercedes received a call from Dave. "The seduced wife called me. She has something to tell you and wants you to come to her home."

"I'm Captain Mercedes. You wanted to talk to me."

Linda let Mercedes in, and after they sat down, "I will do it."

"What will you do?"

"Be kidnapped. I happened to speak to Tyrone and he told me your plan and that he would not do it. I will."

"My boss said it was too dangerous, especially for a woman."

"He's not my boss. I'll do it."

"He won't let me help you."

"Don't tell him."

"How can I do that?"

"Be serious. Have you never kept a secret from a man?

Mercedes smiled. "This is work, but I accept your point. But why? It is dangerous. These guys are killers."

"I would walk through hell to get Tyrone back, or even to forgive me."

Mercedes gasped. "If you're dead, you won't get him back."

"I'll take the chance."

"But you want me to help you take that chance."

"So far you're the only person I know who can make it possible."

"You want me to help you run the risk of getting killed."

"If you see it that way, I can't stop you."

"I do see it that way. And my boss will see it that way. And so will everyone else. The San Francisco police put Linda Neal in danger and she got killed. The only question is after they fire me, will they put me in prison."

Linda started to cry. "This is the first chance I've had to rebuild my life. I'm begging you. Please. It's my life."

Oh my God! "I don't get it. How does this save your life?"

"Tyrone is a wonderful man. I treated him like shit. I hate myself. Especially when I enjoy something, I hate myself. I have no right to joy."

Mercedes stared at her for a long time. On one hand, she was rich, beautiful, and educated. You could say she has everything.

Also, you could see the depth of pain in her soul. It was a tragedy. "Ok, but ..."

"But what?"

"I don't know what. I'm scared. I can see you want this desperately. And as a human being, as a woman, I want to help. I doubt that it's the right thing, but I will try. But we need to work together all the way."

"On my word of honor, I will do whatever you say." Linda started crying again.

"23 points and four three-pointers! You're back man! It's good to have the old Dave back again."

"We are in the playoffs!" They were all slapping Dave on the back. They were all smiles. *I'm glad I'm off that case ... well, at least almost off the case.*

"Tyrone, I need to leave the kids with you for a while. I don't know exactly how long."

"What does that mean? Two or three days, a week, or a month or what?"

"I don't know. I think it will be a few days or a week or two. But I don't know."

"Some new lover boy you're throwing yourself at? The stud you keep at home is not enough?"

"No, it's nothing like that. Let's not fight."

"I'm not fighting. I'm just calling you a whore, which is what you are."

"Tyrone, please, don't! I'm not a whore, and you know that."

"Just a nymphomaniac in heat. I have scars all over me from you. You're a bitch, a bitch who broke my heart."

"I'll bring them over tonight. As soon as I know when I can take them back, I'll let you know. I know you won't believe me, but I'm doing it for us."

"Go to hell!"

CHAPTER 15

A PLAN

Mercedes went to see the chief. "I want to tell you a story. It's all fiction, not a word of truth. But I think at the end you'll agree with me that the story is important."

"Mercedes, I'm busy. I don't have time for stories and games."

"Give me a chance. Please!"

"OK."

"This guy has a sister whom he loves very much, but he knows that she has doubts about how beautiful she is. She has an excellent marriage, but because of her doubts about herself, she is paranoid about her husband. One day she comes to her brother asking for help to test her husband. She wants him to arrange a party and to invite both her and her husband, and another couple. The woman in the other couple will be a paid actress to try to seduce her husband. That way she can test him. And if he passes the test, then she will relax and believe that the marriage is as good as it seems. Her brother knows her husband well and knows that while he is, in fact, deeply in love with her, he is seducible. He tries to talk his sister out of the crazy plan, but she is adamant."

The chief was puzzled. "That's it?"

"Yes, that's it except to ask you what you would do if you were the woman's brother."

"I don't know, and I don't get the point of all this."

Now you will. "If I was the brother, I would arrange the party as requested, but I would also tell her husband the plan. I would not tell my sister that I had told her husband. There is no reason for the brother to risk his sister's marriage just because of her fears. Sometimes, to do what's right, you have to take extraordinary actions, and you have to leave out some facts even when talking to people that you trust. I trust you."

"Is this about the Alteman murder?"

"I think I won't answer that question."

"Professor, this is Mercedes."

"It has been too long. How are you?"

"I'm ok. I miss that surge of pride and excitement I get when I talk to you."

"You're having too much fun with that doctor boyfriend."

"No, no, no. I got rid of him months ago. Too serious and no fun or laughter and I've been through another one since. I'm all free at the moment."

"Why am I blessed with this call?"

"I need your help. It's like nothing else I've ever heard of or that we ever discussed." She explained the case but even more so, the mystery of El Sueño.

"From what you say, the victim, Ted, the Queen, and El Sueño have a relationship with power beyond our understanding. This Linda may be a gutsy lady but she has no real understanding of what she's dealing with."

"Do you?"

"I think I can help you. Can you come to dinner, Friday, say six?"

"I'll be there."

Linda told Mercedes that before she offered herself up to be kidnapped, she wanted to have the best chance of understanding what might happen. They easily agreed that they knew nothing about what to expect. Although it seemed crazy, since the idea had come from Frank Agri, the only thing they could think of was to go and ask him. The women agreed that Linda would go dressed in a very sexy way, so that Frank would not be paying attention to what he said, but rather to her body, while Mercedes went in uniform with her weapon visible so that he knew this was serious.

"Linda has volunteered to be the one to go and visit El Sueño. But we don't know what to expect."

"And why do you want to go?"

"That's my business. It's personal."

"You knew Ted?"

He won't take his eyes off her.

"As I said, it's all personal. I'd rather not discuss it. But I do want to go. And I need some idea as to what to expect."

Frank had his most lascivious sneer. "I know nothing. I'm not sure that I ever met him, but if I did, it was with a lot of other people there at a big resort in Southern California. I talked to him for less than a minute."

"Then how did you know that I can offer to be kidnapped and then meet him?"

"What I do know is that that is how a lot of the people he does business with get to see him. They say he's in the drug trade. But they say he delivers only to intermediaries. He doesn't sell directly. And when he has to make an arrangement about price, or place, or who is the current leader of the group he's selling to, sometimes he has to meet them, face to face, so there are no mistakes. I do know that's how they get to see him. By putting an advertisement out, and then letting themselves be kidnapped."

"And it's safe?"

"Unless you do something stupid. If you bring a gun or try to reverse the kidnap and take the kidnappers, then you get killed. The last guy who was that stupid was a few years ago."

"What was he like when you met him?"

"He looked like a Hollywood cast Mexican. I heard him speak both English and Spanish. He shook hands with a couple of people and smiled. That's all I know."

"Did any of the people who saw him tell you anything?"

"No. They said it was strictly business. But if 'you' go, it'll be anything but business."

Mercedes arranged to pay for the advertisements that Linda was 'available' and then told her the plan was a go. They selected an isolated area just off Highway One, north of San Francisco, as the place for her to be kidnapped.

Mercedes called Dave. "I told you, the chief won't let me go, he wants a man but Neal's wife has volunteered, and he can't stop her."

"What do you want me to do?"

"I want you to be the liaison and her protection."

"I can't help you. She threw me out of her house."

"What?"

"She thought I stared at her because she's so beautiful."

"Did you?" *Men are all the same.*

"Maybe I did, but nothing improper."

"Then it's ok. The plan we got from Agri is she offers to be kidnapped and they will take her to El Sueño."

"That is one hundred percent crazy. She's going to stand on a street corner waiting to be kidnapped? She'll be raped by a pimp in an hour."

"No, a deserted country road. All I need is for you to be there and don't take your eyes off her and make sure she's picked up by the people we want to pick her up."

"How can I know?"

"She will get in the car willingly. If she's resisting, save her."

"Does she know I'll be there?

"I'll tell her."

"Where is this?"

"On a side road off Highway 101 just north of Tomales Bay. I'll send you the details of the time and place by text message."

"Mercedes, you ask a lot."

"I owe you, but we both think this case is special."

CHAPTER 16

TAKE A DEEP BREATH

Caroline, "Solly, it's so good to see you."

"I feel the same."

They embraced, with a long kiss.

"Come on in, and we'll have a drink. Now that Ted's gone, everything is different."

They were both dressed for the date; A mixture of adolescent electricity, almost comical formality, and desire to be attractive. He always wore expensive suits, but this was still more expensive than the others. He had spent some time picking the tie to give him a little color and excitement. It was the middle of the afternoon, but her pink chiffon dress would have been fully appropriate for a cocktail party in the evening.

Solly reverted to his professional voice tone. "The police suspect me. And it is true, I have plenty of motive."

"Did you?"

"No. Did you?"

"No."

Solly smiled, "Perhaps I'm too much of a coward."

"You're not a coward. You are a very good man. And I do love you."

"I guess it's lucky that you are so proper. If they knew how long I've been trying to get you to bed, I'd be in jail."

"No, do they know?"

"No. I lied."

"So did I."

"Well, we'll keep it that way."

"Now I'm not a married woman, just a widow."

"What the police don't know is how respectable you are."

"I had a terrible dream last night. I would call it a nightmare. I saw Ted. He was very nasty. I never saw him anything like that in life. He sneered at me and called me names. He said I was the most sexless woman he had ever been to bed with. He said he was glad to be rid of me. He said that if he was alive today, he'd be grateful to any man who would take me off his hands. All I could do was cry."

"It's not true. You're a good woman, and very attractive. He just played on your fears in life, and now he plays on them after he's gone. I love you."

They embraced and kissed. "Thank you so much. I needed that." She tilted her head with a coquettish smile. "Tell me the truth if you did it?"

"No. God knows I wanted to, but I didn't."

"You wanted to do it for me?"

"I'd love to say yes, but the truth is no. I wanted to do it for me. I want you, as I do now for myself. Maybe I'm not a nice man. Maybe I'm just greedy to get a good woman. But the truth is I would've done it for myself."

"I love you. With all my heart, I love you." Again, they sat in silence. Caroline was almost giddy. "The police made it easy to mislead them. I told them I wasn't jealous of his women. I wasn't. I didn't want him anymore. They could have him. They were foolish like me. They saw his good looks, his money, his energy, and even his skill in bed, but they never saw that he had no heart."

"They tell me he was once a very good man. Very generous and kind. But somehow he changed."

"I've heard the same things about how he was before. And maybe there was even a little bit left when I met him, which made it easy to fall for all the rest. But for almost all of our life together, he was cold and without soul."

"We need to be careful so the police don't have too much temptation to frame us."

It was the end of a long day, and they needed some good news. Dave was sitting in his office, and Martinez was there when Johnny burst in. "They found the gun."

Dave, "Where?"

"In a big trash bin at the hotel that only gets emptied once a month. That's why we just found it."

Dave asked most of the questions, while Mercedes leaned back in authority. "Are you sure it's the right gun?"

"A Ruger LCR, just like we expected."

Mercedes, "Have you traced it?"

"Yes. It was bought in a very high-class gun store in Novato. The buyer was identified as Lucille Walker with an address in Mill Valley. No Lucille Walker lives or has ever lived at that address. We found five Lucille Walkers in the greater Bay Area. One has been semiconscious in a nursing home for months. One will graduate from the eighth grade this year. One moved to Texas a few months ago. I have been trying to arrange to interview the other two."

"Are any of the suspects related or friends with a Lucille Walker?"

"None that we know about, but we are checking further."

"Hospital employees?"

"None that we know about, but we are checking."

"The law firm?"

"The same."

"Any fingerprints?"

"No, clean as a whistle."

Mercedes stood up to leave. "Thanks. It sounds like a good effort. But you've got to push to the max! All hands on deck! The boss wants this case solved, and now!"

Mercedes called Linda. "Tonight is the first night to wait."

"How will I get there?"

"Tonight at midnight, Dave will drive you and drop you off and drive away. He'll park far away and hike back to hide in the woods."

"Thank you, Mercedes. I didn't know you before this, and who knows how it will work out, but you are a true friend"

"I hope to God, it works out. If not, it will be the end of both of us."

"From now on, you are my sister."

"I don't know that I'd do this even for my sister if I had one. But I can see how much you want it, and I can't say no."

"I'm ready."

"Are you? Think one more time. These guys are killers."

"These guys are not stupid. They have no reason to kill me."

"Ok, well wear something loose and baggy so the kidnappers don't rape you."

"Hell no. If they think I'm trash they'll treat me like that and pass me around like a bottle of beer. I will go as a rich bitch. They will think I'm the boss's personal meat and not dare to touch me."

Mercedes laughed. "OK sis. You may be right. At least Dave won't take his eyes off you."

Mercedes felt twelve years old when she walked into the professor's house. It was through this metaphorical door that she had walked from being the child of uneducated Guatemalan peasants into a new modern life. She almost cried when he served her dinner. Then he asked about her life. She looked at him with a little tear in her eye, and said, "I don't know. Some things are very good. I have a good job. I got promoted. I'm going to school and learning a lot. I have great ambitions, and a deep sense of gratitude to my parents and you who have brought me this far. But there are lots of little things that don't seem right."

"Men?"

"How did you know? Do you read my mind?"

"No. You're a young woman and that's a big topic at that stage of life."

"I've seen three men in recent weeks. One was a fellow student in graduate school. I've seen him a few times. He's a nice guy, but just disappointing. Another was a big shot who thought he could manhandle me. I had to draw my gun to get him to leave me alone. And last week I went out with a rich doctor I was fixed up with, who had just gotten divorced, and he was old, fat, ugly, and all he wanted was sex. A total disaster."

"You'll find the right guy, sooner or later, here or there, one way or another."

"I'm sure you're right, but I have to say I keep thinking, over and over again, that I need to make a change." She told him the story of the murder. "This is not like anything else that I have seen in police work. It is not like anything my boss or anyone else has ever seen. It makes no sense. But it seems that there is a mystery behind it."

He reached over and turned on a recording of Beethoven's Grosse Fuge. "I've been listening to this piece, almost all my life. It was written by Beethoven and he said it was amongst his best pieces. But I have never learned to appreciate it. I guess I could be stupid and think that it's Beethoven's fault for writing something so difficult for me and others to appreciate. But we know that's wrong. He knew better than us. The fact that we don't understand what he wrote is our failure, not his. It's the same way with many mysteries of life. You can say you don't understand them. But you can't say nature is wrong to be that way. Or as some would put it, God made a mistake. You must learn to think and feel respectfully about things that are true, but you do not understand. It's my observation, that the smartest people realize that most of the truth is incomprehensible. Only the fools think when they say, 'It doesn't make sense', that they are right and the world is wrong."

"This is policework, not philosophy. Someone murdered him."

"Of all the things you don't know at any one point in time, there is a difference between what you don't know but you could know, and what you can't know. In most of your cases at the beginning, you don't know the murderer or the other guilty party, but you have no doubt that you can know, and after your investigation, you usually do know. And of course, there are scientific discoveries, yet to be made, which are things we all can know, but don't yet know. But beyond that, the question is, are there things that are true, but which are unknowable? And then there is the question of how to relate to that which you can't know. The story you tell me implies that there are elements of this murder that include features which are unknowable."

"Was I supposed to understand that?"

He smiled. "You know my family comes from India. It is a very different world in some important ways. Even the nonbelievers receive a perspective on life that is very different from the modern West. Here, our way of thinking is dominated by science. That which is in science is true and real, and everything else is at best an old wives' tale, superstition, or simply untrue. But in India, there is truth received from the ancient texts, which is invisible to science. Take for example, the idea of reincarnation. If it is true, then there is no scientific way to show that it is true. But there is also no scientific way to show that it is not true. And so that if it is true, Westerners will not believe it, calling it religion or superstition, or some other word. They can call it what they want, but it does not change the possibility that it could be true."

"Professor, as much as I admire you, this a dead man. There is no ambiguity about that. He is already buried. That's a scientific fact. I don't want to deny anyone the opportunity to believe in their religion, but that is not a fact."

"First of all, you are now more than old enough to stop calling me professor. Call me Krishna. But you know there are people who suffer terrible injuries that cause a great deal of pain in almost everybody who has had such an injury. But some of them, who follow the wisdom of the ancient texts, do not have pain. That is a fact."

"Maybe they say they have no pain, but is that really true? If there are damaged parts of their body, they must have pain."

"That's not true. You know with confidence that if you had those injuries, you would have pain. But you have no way of knowing if they have pain. And if they say they don't, that is the only truth there is. You need to expand your way of thinking. We think that the physical reality that we experience, is the only reality there is. But you can invert that, and say that the cycle of birth, life, and death is not permanent, and therefore it is not real."

"I am lost. It seems as if you were saying there is no truth. That there are no facts or reality. Just what anybody wants to say is as good as anything else."

"No. Almost the opposite. All the science is true. All the things that you experience beyond that are true for you. What I'm saying is there are things that can be true that you don't know, that you may never know, and maybe unknowable to any human being. All humans have known that since the beginning of time. They created ideas that some moderns look down upon as religion and superstition. I don't care what you call it. But the arrogance to believe that we are capable of understanding everything and that we understand so much that it is close to everything, that is the error."

"You're saying we may never find the murderer?"

"Yes, and you may want to learn to be content with that. It is just a touch of humility. But in the vastness of life, perhaps there will be balance somewhere."

After dinner Mercedes left and went home, filled with affection for the old man, but no real understanding of what he might've been talking about.

Linda dressed in a floor-length fitted cream-colored gown, with 3-inch heels, a gold necklace, and bracelets. The car pulled over and a man got out of the back seat. "La gata?" That was the agreed-upon codeword. Linda smiled, got in, and found herself seated between two men. One of the men poured a liquid onto a towel and held it up to her face. "Breathe deeply and you will awake with Pablito."

PART II
WHILE IN CHIAPAS

CHAPTER 17

EL SUEÑO

Fog, oh blinding mist, impenetrable.
Fog, warm blanket, protect me.
Fog, confusion without orientation.
Fog, to hide the beasts of prey.
Fog, the comfort of dreams.
Fog, the endless rest of death.
Fog, the innocence of youth.
Fog, leading to fog leading to fog …

"Where am I?"
"That's not for you to know."
"What will you do with me?"
"That's not for you to know."
"What can I know?"
"We shall see."
"I can't see anything."
"Before we let you look out, we want you to look in."
"What does that mean?"
"Who are you?"
"Linda Neal."
"That's your name. We want to know who you are."
"I don't understand the question."

Linda opened her eyes. Her body ached slightly, but the bed was soft. The room was minimally lit, and she began to look around. *I think I'm OK. Nothing's broken.*

"My name is Pablito. Welcome to my home."

Practically no accent. "Where am I?"

"As I said, you are in my home."

He's handsome. Taller than I expected. "And where is your home?"

"In Chiapas, Mexico. Not far from Guatemala."

"What day is it?"

"Thursday. It took them four days to bring you here."

Oh my God. "Four days?"

"What did you expect? It's a long distance from San Francisco to the south of Mexico. Do you have to tell someone that you are safe?"

"Am I safe?"

"Very safe, unless you try to do something stupid. But we would not have brought you here if we thought that you were going to try something stupid."

"Do you know why I'm here?"

"We know only that you must have spoken to someone who has dealt with us before because you asked to come here in the right way."

So far so good. "Do you have many visitors like me?"

"No, we have very few visitors. And none like you. Why did you dress that way?"

"What way?"

"As if you were going to a fancy dress ball. We have very few visitors, very few of whom are women, and none who dress like that."

"I didn't want my kidnappers to think I was common trash or a hooker on the street. I figured if they thought I was a cheap hooker, they would treat me like one and pass me around amongst

95

themselves. If they were going to think of me for sex, I wanted them to think that I was your whore, so they would be afraid to touch me. It seems to have worked."

"That's very clever thinking, but you were never in any danger. We don't rape women under any circumstances."

He sounds safe. "I could not know that, even if it's true. After four days I need to tell the San Francisco police that I am safe or otherwise, they will start searching for me."

"No problem. The telephone is over there on the table. It is set up as a San Francisco number, so you do not have to use any international codes. This is your room while you're here. None of the women here are your size, so we had to buy you some clothes. I hope they fit, and you like them. I'll leave you alone for a few minutes, and then come back." He left.

It was a large bedroom in Spanish colonial style. Linda looked out the window and saw a garden filled with colorful flowers. There was a mirror on the closet. They had changed her clothes, and she was in a somewhat plain dress. She reached underneath and realized this was not her own underwear.

Mercedes told Dave to go to Linda's house and check that everything was OK since she had been gone so long. "And while you're there, check up on her live-in lover."

"I met him for five seconds when I first went to interview her."

"Well check them out for real this time."

"I said I wanted to be off this case."

"Please Dave, I need you."

"You ask a lot."

Dave went and knocked on Linda's door. When George answered in his bathrobe, Dave showed him his badge and asked to come in.

"Mrs. Neal is not here."

"I know. You're her live-in lover. George ... something."

"George Wilson."

"She called you her lover."

"You could say that. I'm more of a boy toy. If I dropped dead tomorrow, she wouldn't even know or care. So, I'm not sure I qualify as a lover."

Even though it wasn't true, he said, "We know where she is. I've been asked to check up on the house while she's gone. I'll drop by every few days."

"Do whatever you want. I don't care."

"How did you meet her?"

"I guess it was shortly after her divorce. She decided to take an art class. I was taking the same class. She's a good bit older than me, but still quite pretty. I decided to try. When I realized how much money she had, I kept trying. I didn't have any other options like her. Eventually, we got together."

"Lucky you," Dave smirked.

"That's the truth."

"Have you heard from her?"

"No. Should I expect to? She's a very tough lady. I do what I'm told when I'm told, and I don't ask questions. She doesn't ask me what I do, and I would never dare ask her what she does. Since I've known her, she's gone away for as much as a couple of weeks and never told me anything. Why should I expect to hear anything now?"

"I don't know. Maybe not until she comes back." *She could be the killer. She's a tough lady, and if she wanted revenge she'd get it. But she's so tough, I don't think she needs revenge.*

Linda dialed from memory, the direct line to Mercedes' office.

"Hi, it's Linda Neal."

"Oh, my God, you're alive! I was terrified they just killed you. I was already trying to make up an explanation for my boss."

"I am alive and unhurt. They have given me a very nice bedroom, new clothes, and the phone I called you on direct to San Francisco. I have met El Sueño. He's good-looking and very polite."

"Oh, my God, what took four days?"

"They told me I'm in Chiapas."

"You're on your own, lady. Chiapas is the other side of the world. We can't help you at all."

"I think I'm quite safe. If they wanted to do something, they would've done it already."

"Are you free to talk"

"I assume they can listen in if they want, but yes, so far, I feel free to say whatever I want."

"Do you think they're listening?"

"I don't know, however, it seems they have no idea who I am or why I'm here. All they know is that I contacted them the right way. We'll see what happens next. If they keep this phone live, I will update you as we go along."

"Good luck."

"Any progress on the case up there?"

"Not really. Everything seems to disappear once you get close to it. I'll tell you all about it when you get back."

CHAPTER 18

WHO ARE YOU?

Pablito returned. "Would you like something to eat? You must be hungry. We couldn't feed you much while you were sleeping or semiconscious."

"Thanks for the new clothes."

He has a woman. "Angela took care of you during the trip. Before she came to us, she was a nurse."

"I don't remember anything from the trip."

"They woke you up just enough to change your clothes and keep you from starving. But we also gave you some scopolamine so that you would not remember."

"I am hungry."

"I think they made carnitas with beans and salad. Is that OK?"

"Sounds fabulous."

After they sat down for lunch, he asked, "Why are you here?"

"Who killed Ted Alteman?"

"Why do you want to know?"

"He was my lover."

"You said *was*. Your relationship with him is over?"

"Yes, but not before he ruined my life."

"So, you're not sad to see him dead?"

"No, I'm not. But his death was very mysterious and my relationship with him was also very mysterious. I've been told that you can answer my questions."

"Perhaps."

"Do you know who killed him?"

"I know everything, and I know nothing. It depends upon what kind of answer you want."

"Do you know who killed him?"

"It depends upon what kind of answer you want."

"I want the name of the person who killed him."

"I can't be sure, but there is probably no answer to that question."

"Can you find out?"

"If there is an answer, I can try, but in all likelihood, there is probably no answer to that question."

"He was alive and healthy and then suddenly he is dead. How did it happen?"

"Why do you care? He's dead and your relationship with him is over. Why do you care?"

"I need to understand myself. I was happily married to a wonderful man, and I threw myself at Ted, over and over again, in the most public and hurtful way to my husband.

When I think back about it now, I can't remember very much, and most of all I can't remember ever liking him. I can't even remember being in lust with him. Nevertheless, it led to my divorce, and it ruined my life. Up until he died, I assumed it was all my craziness. But now he died in a very, very mysterious way, and the police are baffled. So now I think there is something more to know about how I behaved. That's why I'm here."

"I'm sorry to disappoint you, but I and we know nothing about you."

"Who is the queen?"

"That is a question for which there is an answer, but you are unprepared to understand the answer."

"What the hell does that mean?"

"Just what I said. You do not have the experience, training, and perspective, from which to understand what I would say. Therefore, you will interpret the words that I use in ways that I don't mean because that's all that makes sense to you. But you will understand nothing."

"Don't condescend to me. I am well educated and intelligent."

"Far from it. If I felt like condescending to you, I would just say I don't know and send you on your way. But I do empathize with the way Ted destroyed your life. And I do admire your courage in coming here. So, I am treating you with the maximum respect. I'm explaining to you that there are things you do not understand."

What is going on? "I mean no disrespect, but you don't sound like the drug kingpin that I was led to expect. Are you really El Sueño?"

Smiling, "Yes, I really am called El Sueño. I don't know what you were led to expect. People say the stupidest things. It's true that we handle drugs that are illegal. And it's true that we sell some of them to some not very nice people. But we don't go looking for them. We don't go looking for trouble."

"I was told that you, and I guess the people who work for you, held off the entire Mexican army. How is that possible?"

"As I told you, there are things you do not understand, and you are unprepared to understand the answer."

"Teach me."

"Why?"

"I want to understand two things. Most importantly, for myself, I want to understand how, and why I destroyed my marriage. Secondly, and less important for me, I want to understand who killed Ted and how."

"How do you know I won't just rape you and kill you, and then be done with you?"

"To seek what I want, it is a risk I will have to take."

"To give you what you want, will take time."

"I am ready to stay as long as you want. Nothing else is as important."

"I'm impressed."

"Is my phone tapped?"

"No. We have no reason to listen to your conversations. You cannot know anything we don't want you to know. You cannot do anything we do not want you to do. And the rest is your business. That's not the way we work."

I'm in over my head. But there's no turning back. I'll see this through to the end regardless of what happens.

Tyrone knocked on the door. His stomach was turning even before the first knock. This was the house that he had lived in with Linda. George answered the door in his shorts.

"Is Linda home?"

"Who are you?"

"I'm her ex-husband, but I keep in contact and she has not answered for almost five days. She is the mother of my children. I need to know if she's OK."

"I don't need to answer your questions. I don't know that she would want me to answer your questions. Just go!"

"I want to know."

"No!"

"I will not leave until you tell me where she is."

"Then I'll just close the door."

"The hell you will!" Tyrone then just stepped forward and pushed George back. George started to lunge at him. Tyrone hit him with a strong right to the jaw, and George fell down semiconscious. Tyrone stepped around him into the house and yelled, "Linda, are you here? Linda! Linda, where are you?" There was no answer. Tyrone stepped around George again, going to the door, and said, "I'll be back, and don't try to stop me again!"

Later they had dinner, Linda, Pablito, and Angela. They were served by other women. The food was ordinary, enchiladas, beans, rice, and salad, but well-made and tasty. Angela smiled at Linda and said, "I hope you find the clothes comfortable. I had no idea what you would like."

"They're fine. Thank you very much. Pablito said you had been a nurse. I appreciate that you took good care of me on the trip."

"It was my pleasure. We don't get many visitors."

"I was told you fought off the Mexican army."

"They were not invited."

"That's no answer. That doesn't tell me how a few of you here held off an army."

"Why are you here?"

"As I told Pablito, I need to know who murdered my former lover and also, if possible, why I let him be my lover."

"You want us to tell you why you picked a man for a lover? I don't always know why I pick a man for a lover, myself. Attraction is a mystery."

"But I was never attracted. I was crazy. Somehow, somewhere, by some means, someone made me crazy. I would like to know how it happened."

"We all go crazy sometimes."

"This was not ordinary crazy. I was told that you understand mysterious powers. I think I was taken over by mysterious powers." And after a long silence, "Why are you here?"

"I support our work here. It is very important."

"What is that work?"

"You could say that we are the avenging angels of ordinary people. When some things get too far out of balance, we restore some of the balance."

"Was murdering Ted restoring the balance?"

"Maybe. I can't be sure, but maybe."

"Did you murder him?"

"Maybe. I can't be sure, but maybe."

"How can you not be sure if you murdered a man?"

"Maybe I forgot. Sometimes I make an effort to forget things I've done not because I'm embarrassed by what I've done, but because it's convenient. He might've been something I forgot."

"I think you're playing with me. I don't think that's right. I am serious."

"I am totally serious. Pablito respects you and I do too."

"Then tell me a straightforward way, did you kill him?"

"The truth is not straightforward. The truth is complicated, subtle, ambiguous, and includes apparent contradictions. If I answer you in a 'straightforward way' I will be in effect lying. Even as I try to tell you the truth, I will think that the words I give you are misleading because they are straightforward. And much worse, you will think you understand me, when in fact you do not. If you want an honest answer that contains the truth you must accept that it will be very un-straightforward."

After a long silence, Pablito said, "Actually, it is more complicated, even than the way Angela has presented it. She and I play different roles. We have different perspectives. And therefore, some of her facts are unknown to me, and some of my facts are unknown to her. But even the facts that we share, since we have different perspectives, we understand those facts differently."

"I should just give up and go home?"

"You are very privileged. We are conscious that your affair with Ted and his death has had a big effect on your life. We are conscious that you are brave in offering to come here and be totally at our mercy. We are conscious that what we do and why we do it are misunderstood in the world in which you live. Therefore, we let you come here and we will show you the path that we are on if, in addition to your courage, you have the intelligence to open your mind to a world you do not understand."

After a long silence, "I am ready to learn."

CHAPTER 19

I'LL KEEP YOU INFORMED

"It's Linda again."

"What is your impression?"

"He's not that tall but more than I expected. He's a little bit dark, not just in his skin, but also in his demeanor. But I would say he's handsome."

"I told you Linda, you're on your own. If you start falling in love with him it's your problem."

"I'm not falling in love with him, but he is interesting. He doesn't speak like a drug lord. He speaks like a very educated man. He has only a slight accent in English."

"He is a drug lord. He is a killer. Don't let him sweet talk you."

"He's not sweet-talking me. But I do like him. He's not at all what I expected. Most of all, I feel safe."

"Sounds like you're doing better than me."

"What does that mean?"

"I was on a date with a guy who I thought was quite safe. But when I told him to take me home, he kept driving to his apartment. I had to draw a gun on him."

"A gun?"

"A gun. I'm a cop. I know how to use a gun. I often carry one in my purse."

"Oh, my God!"

"Let's hope he doesn't start to play rough."

"He won't. The key thing is not how they look to us, it is how we look to them. They see themselves as good guys. Even on the issue of drugs, they see themselves as just selling stuff to people who want it. They see us, and I think also Ted, in much more ambiguous terms than we think they do. I don't know yet, and maybe I never will, but I think what they would say is that Ted got me because I wanted it, and now he's gotten what he deserves."

"I don't know what to say except good luck."

I'll keep you up to date."

"I love you."

"I love you."

Caroline, still winsome and pretty at age 34, and Solly, fat and gray at age 64, embraced and kissed with all the passion of teenagers in love for the first time. They were safe and alone on the far side of an empty beach. Then they would walk silently holding hands. He would breathe deeply, inhaling her youth, charm, and sexuality. For her, he was a port in a storm. Her traumatized soul just kept leaning in, feeling his strength, and then the most wonderful feeling of all, she relaxed. She stopped, stepped in front of him, and looked straight into his eyes.

"I'm worried Solly."

"About what?"

"Us."

"What do you mean?"

"Now that I'm a widow, now that I'm a free woman, I'm worried things will change."

"In what way?"

"I'm afraid you'll expect things of me that I can't give and I'll expect things you cannot give."

"Why?"

"Because I'm half your age."

"Does that make such a big difference?"

"I can't plan to spend the rest of my life with you. And I don't want to spend the rest of my life alone."

"I'm not dead yet."

"Of course not. And I do love you. I'm very grateful for all the things you've done for me. But I can't plan to spend the rest of my life with you. It's not realistic."

"Let's not discuss it now."

"That's fine. I don't want to discuss it either. But I need to be honest with you. I owe you so much. I can't spoil my relationship by misleading you. I have to make sure you know where I'm at."

Life is continuous, and what's past is past, but not always completely. Little bits can surface later, sometimes to great effect, and sometimes of no meaning.

The mayor's face was uncharacteristically strained. "It's not a secret. A few people know. I'd rather you didn't spread the word at all. But I think under the circumstances, you do need to know. Many years ago, Ted Alteman and I were very close friends. "

The chief immediately adjusted his demeanor to serious and confidential. "When was that?"

"It was about 30 years ago. We were in New York. He had just come back from playing basketball in Turkey, and I was just out of the service. We met in a sports bar. He was already making big money and showing it off to the women. I was extremely fit, having been a Navy Seal and showing it off to the women. We were more than a little wild and crazy. After about a year and a half, it was over. I moved out here to try to start a career, and he stayed there. We were already moving in opposite directions personally. He was outgrowing his fundamentalist religious upbringing. When we first met, he was still more than a little preachy, but by the time we parted that was gone, and when he wanted to, he could even be a bit foul-mouthed and abusive. I was migrating from being a footloose sailor to being a politician. We didn't even keep in touch until he moved out here. And then, because we were both prominent people, we met frequently. But we never talked about the old days. They were gone, and we were completely different people."

"So, this investigation will not uncover any connection between you and him, correct?"

"Not unless you go back 30 years."

"Do you have an opinion about the murder?"

"I know you've picked up some stuff about him having supernatural connections. He did peddle a little of that even back in New York. But I thought then, and I think now, it's just his bullshit."

"I might agree with you that it's not real, but my officer on the case doesn't think so. It's a little non-standard, but one of the women Ted seduced agreed to go to Chiapas to see if she can learn something that applies to the murder."

"The last thing I want to do is to interfere in your investigation."

"And it's the last thing I need to have my mayor looking over my shoulder in the most complicated case I've ever had."

"Over and out to you."

"I'll keep you informed."

CHAPTER 20

WHO KNOWS?

"I had dinner with both Pablito and Angela."

"Now he's now Pablito, not El Sueño?"

"Yes, I think so. He does not want to be called that and so I don't. But also, El Sueño is a drug dealer. That's quite different from Pablito, an educated and interesting man."

"It sounds to me again like you're falling for him."

"He is very charming, but no. I have two children at home. He is staying here, and I am going there. There is nothing to discuss. But otherwise ... maybe."

"That's pretty amazing for a man you just met."

"That's true. There's something about him that is amazing."

"So what have you learned?"

"I learned that Angela is important also."

"Is she his wife?"

"I don't think so. They don't talk that way. Perhaps they are lovers, but I can't be sure."

"What have you learned?"

"Angela might be the killer. She's very important and a very tough lady. I asked her directly if she killed him and she was evasive. She said maybe. She said literally, I might have forgot. It's a little crazy, but I think I'll learn more."

"So what happens next?"

"It's all very mysterious. I'll see what happens tomorrow."

When Mercedes passed on the information about Angela to the chief, he immediately ordered an investigation. But it came up with nothing about anyone named Angela associated with El Sueño. But then there was one lead.

"A woman flying on a Mexican passport arrived at San Francisco airport from Guatemala City three hours before the murder. She had no luggage. She rented a car and returned to the airport six hours later, and left to go to Guatemala City again."

"What's her name?"

"The passport is fake."

"Do we know anything?"

"We have the surveillance pictures. But no identification."

"When Linda gets back, we can see if she can identify the pictures."

After dinner, Linda, Pablito, Angela, and some of the other women all sat together in the large room. There was a nice fire, but relatively little conversation. There were some disagreements on what music to play, but after Angela insisted, it was a series of traditional Latin American romantic songs. When Linda asked Pablito what he was reading, there ensued a brief conversation about Chekov plays. When Linda said that no one would believe her when she told them the famous drug dealer El Sueño was reading Chekov, Pablito corrected her and said, "I am Pablito Mendoza Garcia, a graduate of Yale in comparative literature." He went on, "You know Chekov was a doctor, and he knew how to listen. That's why the most important things in his plays are what is not said."

Perhaps because of all the wine they drank, that night, Linda had a very strange dream.

"Get down on your knees. This is your last chance to beg for mercy before the court issues its judgment."

"But I still don't know what I did. How can you condemn me when I don't know what I did wrong."

"Do not try to play games with this court. You know very well what you have done. You are filled with arrogance, self-importance, and pride. Beg now or accept our judgment that you are not suitable."

"Forgive me. I did not realize that I was so filled with such narcissism. Please tell me what I need to do to set myself right and beg for the mercy of the court"

"Renounce the arrogance of your beauty. Acknowledge your ignorance and pathetic lack of knowledge. Humble yourself and allow yourself to diffuse into the meaning pervasive in all time and space."

"Is this Captain Mercedes Herrera?"

"Yes, what can I do for you?"

"Please wait one second and I'll connect you with Dr. Arigot here in the Marin General Hospital Emergency Department."

After a moment, "This is Dr. Arigot. Am I speaking to Captain Mercedes Herrera in San Francisco?"

"Yes"

"I have to report an assault and battery. I have a young man here, named George Wilson, who was living in the home of Ms. Linda Neal, with her permission when her ex-husband came and beat him up. He now has a broken jaw, a concussion, and perhaps some other injuries that we have not yet identified. Mr. Wilson said that the owner of the house, Ms. Neal, had been working with you on some serious matter and that you would know what to do with this information."

"Thank you. Yes, I am the right person to talk to. I will have an officer there to interview Mr. Wilson as soon as possible."

In all my life, I never expected to walk into a brothel. I never expected to travel all the way to Monterey, Mexico to walk into a brothel. At least I speak Spanish as a native. The Madame looks, as expected, very weather-beaten.

"What do you want with me?"

The perfume is nauseating. "We just want some information."

"I don't give information to the police, and they don't give information to me."

"You don't have to be defensive. I'm not here to bother you. I want your help."

"I don't help the police, and they don't help me."

"We've been told you know the queen."

"And what if I do? What is that to you?"

"We have a murder to solve. It has nothing to do with you. We're not here to bother you. But the little we do understand points for someone very mysterious everyone calls the queen."

"I have nothing to offer you."

"Do you know the queen"

"As I said, I might. But why should I tell you anything?"

"Maybe someday we can help you."

"I don't believe you. The police never keep promises, especially offers to help. But what the hell, tell me what you want?"

"Who is the queen?"

"I don't know. No one knows."

"What do you know?"

"I'm a whore. I've been a whore for a long time. Now I run a whorehouse. That's all I know."

"Who is the queen?"

"Let's start this conversation again. Why are you in such desperate circumstances, that a policewoman comes a long distance and asks for help from an old lady who runs a whorehouse?"

"I've been told that you're a lot smarter than you let on. You're right. I have a problem that I can't solve. I need to know, who is the queen?"

"The queen is street talk. The queen is Lady Luck. The queen is the voice you hear when you're drunk or asleep or doing something else stupid."

"There's got to be more to it than that. People say that the queen can have people killed. People say the queen defeated the Mexican army. There's got to be more to it than that."

"When I was a little girl, I was a good little girl. We went to church every Sunday. I was told that God would reward me for being good. It wasn't true. Lots of things happened."

"I don't get it. What does that mean?"

"It means that when things happen to you and you don't know why, you gotta have a reason. When I was little, the reason was God. I let a boy take off my panties, and I got the punishment I deserved. But I didn't deserve it. So why did I get punished?"

"Life's not fair."

"That's it. Lots of things happen that make no sense. If you don't want to call them God, then call them the queen, or luck, or something else I don't know what. I'm a whore it's all I know."

"Have you seen the queen?"

"No."

"Have you talked to the queen?"

"No."

"Has the queen ever done you a favor?"

"You could say so. One time when I was very young, and my pimp beat the shit out of me, I cried all night, begged in my soul for vengeance, and wished he was dead. The next day he was dead. Maybe it was just luck, but for me, it was the queen giving me justice."

"That's it?"

"Things like that have happened to me many times in my life. I believe it was the queen. And I know others, with similar luck, who believe it was the queen."

"And have you done things for the queen?"

"Maybe I have. Some men have come here who behave like bastards here, or I found out behave like bastards elsewhere. Somehow their wives, or their bosses, or the press, or someone found out. No one can be sure how they found out. I don't say I did it, but I do say the queen would be pleased if she knew."

"Do you know El Sueño?"

"Years ago. He was just a kid then. I helped him."

"Do you think he knows the queen?"

"That's a stupid question. No one can answer that."

"What do you think of him?"

"He was a wonderful person as a kid, and I know he's a wonderful person now even though I haven't seen him for years."

"How do you know?"

"I know the people he's helped."

"They say he's a drug dealer and that he's killed men."

"I'm sure he has."

"Then how can you know he's a wonderful person?"

"I just do."

CHAPTER 21

FIRST LESSONS

The following morning, after breakfast, the sun was shining. Pablito asked, "Would you like to go for a walk?"

"Whatever you say."

"There is a beautiful trail to the top of the mountain. It is a little steep but the view is spectacular."

"Let's do it."

Shortly after they started the walk, "What was the most humiliating experience of your life?"

"That's a weird question. Why do you ask?"

"You want me to teach."

"I don't know if this is what you want. When I had finished my first year in high school, and I had done very well, my parents gave me a trip to visit my uncle, my mother's brother, in Paris. My uncle was ten years older than my mother and immediately after college he went into finance, became quite rich, and had not lived in America all that time. My mother's first husband, my biological father, was a sergeant in the army. She divorced him when I was six, and remarried the man who raised me, who was a high school history teacher. Not a lot of money there. So, it was a big deal when my uncle offered to pay for me to visit him. For many years he had not married, although my mother said he had had a lot of girlfriends. But now, almost sixty, he had married a woman in her

116

twenties and had two preschool children. She was a very dynamic and beautiful woman, an attorney with her own career, and they seemed, and as I got to know, were, and still seem to be, extremely happy together. One day, it was announced that my aunt had a case in Germany, Aachen if I remember correctly, and would be away for the weekend. On Friday, my aunt got a phone call, and she was clearly startled and moved immediately to the next room and started speaking in German. What she did not know, and for that matter neither did my uncle, is that my mother's first husband had been stationed in Germany just before the divorce, and I had learned German very well. I could hear my aunt's side of the conversation. It was a call from her lover, changing the details of where they would be spending the weekend together. She came back into the room and acted as if it was nothing, and so neither did I. However, the following week, when we were alone in the kitchen, I started to speak German to her. She laughed, was pleased, and commented on how rare it was for Americans to have language skills. Then, after about five or ten sentences, she realized the significance and just stared at me. I of course regretted being smart-assed, just stood there, and finally, thinking of nothing else to do, I smiled. It probably wasn't very long but it felt like an eternity, she just stared. Then she smiled and said, 'He doesn't know.' I told this story once to my ex-husband and you are the second."

"We can start with this. Do you have many secrets?"

"No, I don't think so, except during the affair from Tyrone."

"And have many people had secrets from you?"

"How would I know?"

"That you learned of later."

"Tyrone bought me an extremely expensive necklace for our first anniversary. At the time it was much more than even he could afford at that moment. Years later I saw our accounts. He had borrowed the money. I only learned the truth during the divorce. Every time I think about it, including now, I hate myself."

"So, in your first story, you knew, and came to know, facts others did not. In this story, other people knew things you did not."

"Yes, so?"

"Your uncle has so far, as far as you know, lived happily ever after, deluded in ignorance of his wife's infidelity."

"Why should I have destroyed a happy marriage?"

"What if one or both of the children are not biologically his?"

"Then he's lived happily without the truth."

"What would you think if I decide you would be happier without the truth of Ted's death?"

"I hope you don't. I want to know what happened to me."

"People always say they want to know the truth. But the truth is, they usually don't want to know the truth. As you decided for your uncle, they are often better off with comfortable delusions."

"Who gets to decide?"

"I will decide how much truth it is appropriate to give you."

"And how will you make that decision?"

"It depends on you. If I think you can understand what you're told, I will tell you more." He looked into her eyes and petted her hair. "I think you will be able to understand fairly well."

"Who is El Sueño?"

"El Sueño is the name given by the Mexican government, and the popular press, to portray a drug lord living in a well-defended citadel on a mountain in Chiapas State. I am not El Sueño, and he is not me. I am Pablo Mendoza Garcia."

"Who is Pablo Mendoza Garcia?"

"I was born to a relatively well-off petroleum engineer in Veracruz. I am 45 years old. Never married. I graduated from Universidad Nacional Autónoma de México and got a master's in comparative literature from Yale."

"When did you decide to go into the drug business? To become a criminal?"

"I didn't make that decision. It was made for me by the government of Mexico, with more than a little help from the queen."

"That sounds like a cheap excuse. I don't know you, but it already sounds beneath you. The men I admire don't blame others for their lives, and especially not women."

"You misunderstood. I did not blame the Mexican government. I was a very outspoken youth, and I made quite a few enemies, including some very powerful ones. To get even, they framed me for a drug deal in which I was not involved. Such things are common. The Mexican government bought the lie. And the queen is not a woman, or for that matter any human being. Although she did appear to me that day as a woman. When I realized how well I had been framed, and how impossible it was for me to avoid prison, I went for a long walk in the night. I honestly don't remember exactly what happened. Maybe I just fell asleep or got confused and delirious. But I was visited by the queen. She told me she cared for me. She told me not to go to prison and that she would take care of me. I ran away to this spot, and I have been here ever since. While I have been here the queen has shown me truth beyond my imagination and taken care of me with such warmth and generosity, as to earn my undying love."

"Do you want me to believe that?"

"I don't care. It is the truth and I told you because you asked. Who are you?"

"You know already. I'm a middle-aged divorced woman living in the Bay Area."

"It's not an answer. Who are you?"

"I was born Linda Susie Carter in Crab Mountain, Tennessee, 36 years ago. I was 16 years old when Tyrone Neal came home to visit his family after having established himself with a big law firm in San Francisco. He said I was beautiful and smart, and that he was in love with me. He offered to marry me, and as crazy as it may sound, he did. As soon as we got to San Francisco, he arranged for me to start college. I got a first-class education, gave birth to two children, and lived better than any princess on earth until I became an ungrateful bitch. Now that you know my story, and I know that you are not El Sueño, who are you? Who is Pablo Mendoza Garcia?"

"I have killed three men personally. When I first got here, they thought I was an upper-class wimp and so they tried to rob me, etc. Since I have established myself, I have ordered the killing of 12 men. I am a very non-violent man. I only do what I have to do to maintain myself. But life here is not all that I wish it was. My family cannot visit me, and of course, I cannot visit them. Also, although many of the women here are attractive and sweet, there are none that I could form a lasting relationship with since most are uneducated. And unlike Tyrone, when he brought you to San Francisco, I cannot send them to college here."

"You've had a lot of girlfriends?"

"Yes."

"Angela?"

"She is not my lover."

"Was she?"

"I choose not to answer."

"And you?"

"Until Ted came along, Tyrone was the only man I had slept with. Since the divorce, I have had a few, but nothing remotely serious."

"So you are not promiscuous, but who are you?"

"A broken woman desperate to save her life. It is one thing to have your life destroyed by forces beyond your control, but quite another thing to have destroyed yourself. I am by all accounts, beautiful, smart, educated, strong, healthy, and the mother of two beautiful children ... And I am guilty and filled with self-loathing." After a pause, "Who killed Ted?"

"As I've tried to explain, that is not the simple question you think it is."

"What is so complicated about the name of a murderer?"

"That is what you have come to learn. What you know and what you don't know. What is known to some but not to others. What is known to at least someone and that which is still not known to anyone. And finally, and most importantly, that which is knowable to even one person, and that which is eternally unknowable to anyone."

He seems more of a philosopher than a drug dealer. As they climbed higher, the path was in some places a little rough. He would hold his hand out and help her, and after that, they would walk holding hands for some distance. *He is very charming.* When she got tired, they would stop and rest.

"People often say things like, 'I don't know that', about something that they are confident they could know if they wanted it, like calculus. They even say things like, 'we don't know that', or 'that's not known', about things like whether there is extraterrestrial life. They understand everything about it, except whether it's true. But then there are things that are unknowable by anyone by any means known today. But they could be true. You are here to learn about things that are unknowable, but still true. And the first hard part is to learn how to talk intelligently when you literally do not know what you're talking about."

My head is spinning. "I had a very weird dream the other night. Did you give me a drug?"

"Dreams are important. I have dreams at night when I am asleep, but also during the day, when I am wide awake. Some of those dreams, especially the ones at night make no sense and are easily forgotten. But some are extremely powerful, life-transforming, and have a meaning that you carry with you all your life. I understand that not everybody, in fact, only a few people, have such dreams. But if you are one of those people, then you are marked for life."

"How can you tell who has had such dreams and who has not?"

"You can't. You can't tell that I have had such dreams by any means except that I tell you. I have met a few people who have had such dreams, and I could not tell until they told me, I have also met a few who have had such dreams, and I could not tell, but I was told in my dreams that they had had similar dreams, and I have no doubt."

"It's starting to get crazy. No one knows anything."

"No. Once you have either experienced the dreams yourself, or you have been shown a person who has the dreams and you know they've had the dreams, then you can begin to see the telltale signs just by watching. Although I have never seen him, from what you tell me, I am sure that your lover had such dreams."

"How can you tell?"

"Those dreams are communications with the queen. When you see people react or do things that are both powerful and otherwise incomprehensible, it may be the telltale sign of the queen."

"Who is the queen?"

"The queen is not a person or a thing. The queen is just a word that we have learned to use to refer to powers and effects we do not understand. I, and other people who are in communication with what we call the queen, get feelings or ideas that seem to come from nowhere. If we respond appropriately to those communications, then we may establish a pattern where we receive more and more of them. That is my situation. I get ideas and feelings that seem to me come from nowhere daily or more frequently."

"Some men have said they had sex with her?"

"Then that is how they remember it. I have no idea what they mean."

"You think that Ted was in communication with the queen?"

"Yes. When you are in communication with the queen, then at times they use their power to help you. That's what defeated the Mexican army that attacked us here. I don't always understand the reasons that the queen has for what they do. Other people, who do not understand, call it luck, or fate, or divine intervention, or some other word. But by any word, all it means is that they do not know. And in some cases, they are very resistant to even admitting that they do not know."

"I'm confused."

"That's good. If you thought it was clear, it would mean you misunderstood. First of all, whatever the queen is, it is not unitary. It is not one mind, with one purpose, with one action, or with one goal. The image I have in my mind is that there are many civilizations out in the universe that have the power to project into us. There is no reason to believe they agree with each other, or even communicate with each other. Only that they all have the power to put ideas and thoughts in our minds that we do not understand. They do not control us. They are not all-powerful. But they are very powerful at any one thing if and when they choose."

"Are you saying they put it in his mind to commit suicide? That's not possible. He was murdered with a gun."

"No, I'm suggesting that he was in communication with the queen and that's what made him so effective in the things that he did. Probably, the big thing is to put ideas into other people's minds that helped him get what he wanted."

"You mean they drove me crazy towards him?"

"No, but something like that."

"Why?"

"I have no idea. It might've been a mistake. They do make mistakes. Or more exactly, they seem to do things that I think are mistakes. Perhaps they have some reason beyond my understanding."

"Why me?"

"I'm sure they did not choose you. Ted chose you, but perhaps they found some things in you, that were there before Ted, but which they could boost and make you vulnerable."

"I did think at times that I had married too young, and had missed out on something. I can't blame them for the affair. Whatever they did, it was all my volition."

"Absolutely! In the beginning, and in the end, we are each responsible for what we do."

After they walked a little further, they came to a clearing with a view of the valley.

My head is spinning. I don't know how to wrap my mind around what he says. Maybe he's just playing with me. He seems sincere. He seems very nice. The view is gorgeous. My head is just spinning.

When he started to kiss her, she did not resist. And when he started to undress her, she helped him.

CHAPTER 22

THINGS DISAPPEAR

It was the middle of the day, and the widow was sitting in her garden. Perhaps surprisingly for some, she was immaculately dressed in an off-white summer dress and decked out with jewelry. When the phone rang, she immediately, of course, recognized Solly's voice. "Caroline, do you realize that you are nearly broke?"

"Oh no. I never looked at the accounts. Ted took care of everything. Where did it all go?"

"Well, not really broke. For most of the world, you're still extremely rich. But compared to the amount of money you had even a few months ago, it's nothing." Caroline started to cry. "I'll come right over."

As soon as he entered, they kissed. He petted her hair and they went into the garden.

"What can I do?"

"I'm not supposed to know any of this but since some of his accounts were linked to the group practice, I could of course see those, and even though they're not supposed to, they did let me see his other accounts.

"Maybe he has others that our bank doesn't know about."

"Ted withdrew about half a million from your accounts the day he was murdered. Do you know where that money is?"

"No. I always thought we had a lot more money than that."

"He has been spending money at a very high rate for the last few years. From what we've seen as recently as a few years ago, you were indeed extremely wealthy."

"What did he spend it on?"

"I don't know. I'm sorry to say this, but if you've made me guess, he has another woman, or women, elsewhere. And I wouldn't be shocked if he was married to some of them."

"He can't do that."

"People do a lot of things that they can't do and I'm sure that Ted did more than most."

"Can you trace the money?"

"No. Most of it was withdrawn as cash, and the rest sent to secret accounts."

"Can we find out about the secret accounts?"

"It depends upon the instructions he gave the bank. Of course, if he listed you as his wife, etc., then there's no problem. But you have to consider the possibility that he was preparing to leave you. And if there are other names on the accounts, it might not be yours. Like I said, it might be he had another wife somewhere else."

"What am I to do?"

"First of all, it's a matter for the police. They are supposed to find the killer, and they are supposed to find the money. They don't seem to be doing a very good job of either. I can't help much in finding the killer, but I think I can do a lot in finding the money. The real question is in what form is the money now? If he used it to buy a house in Brazil for his other wife, you can probably get it back. The money he put into the house is still value in the house. But if he spends it on fine wine and women, it's gone. There's no way to get it back. But it's hard to spend that kind of money on consumables. If he made an investment, it depends on how the investment is doing. That may have something to do with why he was killed."

"Why should an investment get him killed?"

"Things are worth what people think they're worth. It's the judgment of the market. If you think a new invention will make a lot of money, you might spend a lot of money to buy it. But if the market isn't interested, then the money you invested is gone."

For the rest of the time, she whimpered, and he tried to console her.

Mercedes told the chief that she had something important to tell him, but if possible, it would be better if the mayor was there. "As big as the case is, it's getting bigger." He arranged a meeting an hour later in the mayor's office.

"Gulov is dead."

The mayor was confused. "Who?"

"Sergei Mikhailovich Gulov, that super-rich Russian who knew the queen."

The chief immediately realized the implications. "He's dead?"

"He died in an airplane crash last night. It was his private jet with just the pilot, him, and a girlfriend."

"Where did it happen?"

"Over the North Atlantic, about two hours out of New York on its way to Moscow."

"Do we know why it crashed?"

"No. By all accounts, the weather was clear, and there was no known problem with the airplane. The pilot was very experienced. One report I read suggested that the plane blew up in midair."

"Then why?"

"We don't know. There is not much chance of getting the flight recorder from the bottom of the Atlantic Ocean."

"Do they think he was murdered?"

"That's what the aviation people think."

"Who?"

"We don't know. There is a rumor that he was in trouble with the power centers in Moscow. And then there are his business partners in the drug business."

Then the other shoe dropped for the mayor. "It could be linked to the Alteman murder?"

"Exactly! I think both murders were committed by the same people. Both murders were committed by very sophisticated means. Whoever or whatever is behind them is very powerful and very smart."

"Angela, it looks like I'm going to be here for at least a few days. I appreciate that you took good care of me, and I appreciate the clothes you got me, but to be honest they're not my style."

"What do you want?"

"I'm not Mexican and I think wearing these kinds of Mexican clothes is dishonest. Can you get me something more American?"

"I'll see what I can do. Do you want jeans or skirts?"

"Yes, especially jeans."

"I'll see what I can do."

"And one more thing. Can you tell me more about the murder?"

"Not now. Perhaps another time."

"Please. I need to know."

"What do you want?"

"Did you do it? Do you know who did it?"

"I can't answer questions like that."

"Why not?"

"Because that's not the way we live or the way we work."

"As best as you can, did you do it?"

"OK. I might have done it but I can't be sure. I do remember a trip to San Francisco and back rather quickly. I do remember that I had an assigned task. But I took scopolamine on the way back, and I don't remember any details."

"You really don't remember?"

"Whatever memory I had after I got back, I chose to forget. Now it's all gone."

"We're talking about a murder. That's not nothing. How can you not remember a murder or why you did it?"

"I'm told you were here because you had an affair with the dead man and you don't remember why. Going to bed with a man is not nothing. Going to bed with him multiple times is certainly not nothing. And you don't remember why you did it."

I'm not gonna get anywhere this way.

"My name is Dr. Jenny Moore. I'm told you want to talk to me."

"Please come in. I'm Captain Mercedes Herrera and we are investigating the murder of a man I believe you knew."

"I know that you spoke to my husband, so you know all about it. Why do you want to talk to me?"

"I don't want to be intrusive into your private life, but we understand that you had an affair with him."

"As I said you spoke to my husband, so you know all about it. What do you want from me? The dates? The places? Exactly who did what?"

"Of course not. Ted Alteman was a very strange and unique man. He had relationships with several women, and they all describe it in very strange ways. Especially how it started. I think that's what we want to know the most."

"I don't know that I even remember how it started. I came up from Palo Alto to the city for a meeting. I think it had something to do with medical legal issues and so he was there. Maybe he was one of the speakers. I really don't remember. I vaguely remember agreeing to go out and have a drink with him. And I think the affair started that night. I think I went to his hotel room. He called me a couple of days later and we did it again. And for a while, it was quite intense, but then it died. It's strange, but it seems very far away, almost alien."

That word again. "Did you feel guilty?"

"I do now, but in all honesty, I don't think I did at the time. It was a little bit of a blur. Luckily, my husband didn't find out until it was already over."

"Who ended it?"

"I think I did but he was already not as attentive as he had been."

"One woman has said that she doesn't remember even liking him. Just that she couldn't control herself, as if he had some special power."

"Sounds to me like she's just making excuses."

"No, she feels very guilty."

"Well, I'll admit to something like that. It seemed like a lot of fun, and sexy at the time, but in retrospect, I don't remember why."

"We're trying to learn more about how he operated. Do you have any letters or gifts or anything else that he gave you? He was spending a huge amount of money."

"I didn't need his money or anything. He did spend quite lavishly when we went on trips. But I have no records of that. He did write me letters and give me gifts. But when my husband found out, I burned all of it ... every last scrap!"

CHAPTER 23

MAYBE YES, MAYBE ...

Dave rang the bell at Tyrone's house. "You broke his jaw."

Tyrone slumped. "I'm sorry. I didn't go there to hurt him." Tyrone let Dave into the house and they sat in the living room. "But for a moment, I thought that he might have hurt her. I'm an attorney. I take responsibility for what I did. You've come to arrest me?"

He's a standup guy. I like him. "That's what I was sent to do. But I'm not going to. Years ago, my wife was screwing around behind my back, and it still drives me crazy. I understand where you're coming from. If I can, I will just make this case disappear. I do recommend that you pay for Mr. Wilson's medical expenses."

"Can you really make an assault and battery go away?"

"I think so. My captain will support me. Part of the problem is that we are handling this case in a very irregular way."

"I'm still really rather conflicted about her. I hate her. I hate her from the bottom of my soul for what she did to me. But also, I can't get it out of my head."

"Believe me, I've been there."

"I hate her. She's a dirty filthy bitch who doesn't know anything at this point, except how to spread her legs in front of some man. She's a nymphomaniac and a whore. I hate her."

"Like I said I've been there. Once you've been in love with them, it's hard to get over. And it's especially hard to think of them fucking another guy. But the law doesn't understand that. The law doesn't think you have a right to break his jaw."

"Do you believe you can make my assault just go away?"

"I'll be back in a few days and tell you what happened."

"It's Linda again."

"Everything OK?"

"Yes and no. The situation here is crazy. He is a killer. He told me about 15 people he killed. But I have to tell you he's one of the most charming, intelligent, and interesting men I have ever met. In another life, I would fall in love with him."

"It sounds like I'd like to meet him."

"You would. He's a very attractive man."

"And he's not married?"

"No. He said he has never been married. And it seems he has no special girlfriend, including Angela."

"After this is over, invite him up to San Francisco so I can meet him."

"As you know that's quite impossible. If you want to meet him, you'll have to come here."

"I can't do that. What have you learned about the murder?"

"Nothing for sure. When I asked her, Angela was evasive but said she might have done it. I don't know, but I think I will. I have to gain their confidence, but it's crazy. Sometimes they talk in riddles. When I ask Pablito a question, he answers, 'I know everything, and I know nothing.'"

"I don't know what to say, except keep in touch. The pressure to solve this case is immense. But be careful. Please be careful. I don't want your life on my conscience."

"I will be. But thank you for the concern. It's all very weird. He talks of the queen as a kind of god-like force beyond human understanding, but like God interfering in human lives."

"By the way, there's one other thing. Your ex-husband beat up your live-in boyfriend. He broke his jaw. Your ex apparently just wanted to check up on you, either out of jealousy or love. It doesn't matter. It's a felony assault."

"Oh my God. It was love, not jealousy. It sounds crazy to say, but it's the best news possible."

It was a beautiful California evening, so after the movie, Steve and Mercedes decided to walk back to her apartment. They held hands, smiled, and laughed.

"We are lucky to live in such a beautiful part of the world."

"That's for sure. But in the end, it makes us lazy. We don't ask the deep questions or address the hard problems."

"Like what?"

"Like what am I going to do with my life? It's a more pressing question for women. The clock on making babies is always running."

"Do you want me to get you pregnant?"

"Thank you but no. You're a nice guy, but I'm not ready to settle down with you for the rest of my life."

"I understand. I'm not ready to settle down either."

"And therefore, if you got me pregnant, I'd be a single mother, and that's not right or fair to the child or even to me."

"We're both studying history to understand more. Isn't that important?"

"I do it because I want to understand, but I already have a career as a cop." When they reached the apartment, they stopped and kissed. "If you want to come upstairs with me, it's OK."

"What do you want in a man?"

"I don't know. I don't even know why I want a man. It just seems the natural thing to do. In the modern world, you don't need them for anything. And let me tell you from a woman's point of view, most of them are more trouble than they're worth. Nevertheless, every day I think I should have one. So I keep looking."

"You need them to make babies."

"Not really. It's easy enough to take the sperm and dump the guy. That's probably what I'll do someday."

Dave and Mercedes went to brief the chief. Dave went first. "Gonzalez left the gun behind a trashcan in the back of the hotel, where the victim was murdered the previous day. However, he was in a hospital at the time of the murder after he was beaten up badly in a drunken brawl."

"How did he know where to put it?"

Mercedes, "We don't know. Whoever organized the plot either had Frank tell him, but Frank says he doesn't remember anymore, or more likely, he told Gonzalez directly. They're separate parts of this plot. First, Frank, for reasons we don't know, or if we do make no sense, gets the money and distributes it, possibly with instructions to Gonzalez. Second, Gonzalez gets the gun and also puts the money with instructions under the door of a hooker. Third, she arranges to turn off the monitoring system. Fourth, the cowgirl arranges for Ted to meet her in the hotel. Fifth, the actual killer collects the gun, commits the murder, drops the gun, and leaves. Then, maybe the killer or someone else cleans up the body and dresses it in fresh clothes, and cleans up the room. It seems possible that none of the five principles, Frank, Harry, the hooker, the cowgirl, and the actual killer ever see each other, or have any contact with each other. And to make matters worse, the only suspect with a motive and the capacity to produce such a plot,

Gulov, the Russian oligarch, is now dead himself, probably murdered."

Dave had told Mercedes again that his wife had made it clear that he had to be off the case. Mercedes nodded as if she accepted that, but in her mind, she did not. Nevertheless, she did not ask Dave to go to see the widow. She went herself. Caroline let Mercedes into the house, and they sat in the living room.

"I'll come straight to the point Mrs. Alteman. We have proof that you lied to us."

"I don't know what you have, but you are wrong. I did not lie."

"We have extensive travel documents of your husband over the last few months before he died. He took many trips to some very fancy places outside the country, and on all of them, you were with him. Immigration documented your exit and entry into the country. The hotels where he stayed also have you registered."

What is she talking about? "I don't know what you have, it's not true. You had better look at those documents more carefully. Either you've done very sloppy work, or someone is trying to frame me. I made no trips with my late husband out of the country to any resorts in the last year."

"That won't sell. Why should anyone frame you? And the immigration procedures are very careful."

"Are you going to arrest me?"Maybe."

"Let me assure you, Captain Herrera, that your information is wrong. If you arrest me, you will only embarrass yourself."

"Then how do you explain those documents?"

"I can't. But as I think you have come to understand, my late husband was a very unusual man. He did things differently and beyond what ordinary people do. Perhaps he was traveling with some other woman. I don't think it's a secret that he had girlfriends."

"That's true. We know that."

"Are you going to arrest me?"
"Not yet."

"Vitaly Ramashvilli."

Mercedes was sitting in her office when the phone rang. The connection was poor and she missed half of what was said. "Let's start this conversation again. Who are you?"

"I don't want to tell you. If you don't want my information that's your problem. I'm giving you free information and you can do with it what you want."

"And what is this information you were giving me?"

"Vitaly Ramashvilli, an Israeli Georgian gangster, and part of the same group as Gulov. He had sworn to people I know that he would kill Ted Alteman because of the case where he got $1 billion."

"If you won't give me your name, where are you calling from?"
"Israel."

"And why are you giving me this information?"

"Ramashvilli is a pig. He has killed half a dozen people. I don't know why we can't deal with him ourselves, but we don't. I'm hoping you will give him what he deserves."

"And where would we find him?"
"In Tel Aviv. It's not hard."

"And why are *you* giving me this information?"
"He beat up my sister."

CHAPTER 24

DREAMS

Perhaps there was something in the drink that Pablito had given Linda just before she went to sleep, but although she went to sleep quickly, she had a dream like nothing she had ever experienced before.

"Ted?"

"You seem surprised"

"You are dead."

"I am."

"Then how can I see you?"

"I'm in your dreams.

"You're dead."

"I know."

"I don't understand."

"Do you want to ask me a question?"

"Who killed you?"

"I don't know."

"Can you tell me anything about it?"

"I went to the hotel room. Shortly after I was in the room, there was a knock on the door. I opened the door and she shot me. That's all I know."

"Did you know who she was?"

"No, I had never seen her before."

"Why did you go to the hotel?"

"You have to understand the way they do things. I got a call from a woman I was interested in and she said that she would be available that night. I had worked with them all my life and so I got the feeling they wanted me to go. I had a suspicion I was being set up, but I went."

"Did you know you were in danger of being killed?"

"I knew they were unhappy with me. I had been doing things they didn't like, like seducing you."

"Who are they"

"They are the power that comes from beyond light."

"What does that mean?"

"It means that everything we know, everything the whole human race knows, is nothing. Everything we know must come to us as information through light. But that does not mean that that's all there is. There is the universe beyond the light that reaches us. There are portions of reality that exist outside of the physical universe. There is no way to understand them. But if you give yourself to them, they will do things through and for you that no human being can do."

"That sounds spooky. It sounds crazy. Are you just trying to make a fool of me again?"

"No. I am dead. I have no reason to tell you anything but the truth, as I know it. That is why they are letting me talk to you because they want you to hear the truth."

"I don't know what all that means. These are people who live in some distant galaxy?"

"Maybe, I don't know. All I do know is that when I was still in college, I began to have feelings, unlike anything else in the world."

"That's just a teenager getting drunk."

"I wasn't drunk. I didn't drink. I was raised very strict. I was very religious. That was all gone when I met you, but I was anything but drunk."

"So what happened?"

"The big thing was when I was in Turkey playing basketball. I took some drugs there that showed me a different world. A world beyond my imagination. A world filled with power and color like I have never seen before. My father taught us that the power comes from Jesus, but that's not true. The power comes from beyond light."

"So you went crazy on drugs. Is that it?"

"I didn't go crazy. I came back to America, made money, and did God's work in my own way."

"When was hitting up on me God's work?"

"No. Things change slowly over time. But the drugs gave me a feeling of mystery, of power beyond understanding. When I let myself open up to those feelings, I felt that I got messages from them. Those messages said they would help me, and they did. Things began to happen in my life, that could not be explained in any ordinary way. I guess I could have believed that they were God, but that was not my way by that time."

"Like what?"

"I became a basketball star. I found that a lot of girls were interested in me when I made no effort. As a lawyer, I won some cases where I thought I had a weak position. The most amazing was getting millions of dollars."

"What went wrong?"

"I started to do things that I wanted and that they thought were excessive. They were very angry at the huge amount of money I got. They were particularly upset that I thought it was my skills and not the powers that they had let me use. Similarly, all the other women that I had, wanted me even more than I wanted them. A large part of that, of course, was that I looked good as a result of the powers they gave me, but I did not use that to get the women. As time went on, and I saw a woman I wanted, I did use the power. And once you get used to using the power, it's easier to use it again, and again. I did use those powers to get you."

"They had you killed because you seduced me?"

"I think so. I think they felt that even if it was wrong that I made so much money, most of the people I beat had it coming. They did not see what you had done to deserve to be subverted that way."

"You were in love with me?"

"No, I was in lust with you. By that time, I was quite predatory in many ways. You were beautiful and I wanted you. I got them to use their power to take control of your mind. I don't want to offend you, but as a person, you never mattered."

"You destroyed my life to have a little fun, fucking a pretty woman and then you threw me away."

"That's about right."

"You filthy bastard. They should've tortured you first."

"Linda, you look so beautiful!"

"I must admit, you look familiar, but I don't remember your name or where we've met before."

"In Maui, two years ago. How can you forget? I'll never forget."

"Maybe vaguely. Remind me."

"There was a terror alert in Honolulu, and all the planes were diverted to Maui. We were stuck there for three days. It was a chance meeting, but three of the most memorable days of my life."

"I think I remember, but it feels almost alien to me. Like it did happen, and it didn't happen at the same time."

"I guess I'm forgettable, but you are not. I remember every square inch of your body like it was yesterday."

"Who are you"

"I am the answer to your questions."

"Why can't I see your face?"

"Because I'm not a person with a face."

"Then what are you?"

"As I told you, I am the answer to your questions. If we could understand each other, then you will have the opportunity to meet the power."

"My question is who killed Ted?"

"If you do well, then you will understand the answer to your question."

"You killed Ted?"

"I am the answer to other questions."

"So what questions are you the answer to?"

"I am your opportunity to move to a higher level."

"What does that mean?"

"As you have seen, Pablito, Angela, and others have had experiences that change their inner nature. They think you are sincere."

"I am sincere. And I am serious. I want to understand what happened to me, who killed Ted, and as much of the mystery as you will let me."

"You have started well."

CHAPTER 25

DAMAGE CONTROL

When Tyrone answered the door, Dave said "May we come in?"

"Of course."

Dave and George Wilson walked in, and Tyrone showed them to the living room. "I brought Mr. Wilson with me so that you could apologize."

Tyrone answered slowly, and with obvious feeling. "I do apologize, very sincerely. There is no excuse ... no excuse whatsoever."

Wilson, "I didn't want to come here. He had to practically threaten me. I don't like having my jaw broken. But I do understand the pain women can cause. I'll try to get over it."

"Thank you again. Believe me, the apology is totally sincere. I assume the officer told you that I am more than happy to pay for any expenses I've caused."

Wilson nodded.

"Where is she?"

Wilson, "I don't know."

Dave, "I don't know either. I do know she is on some incredibly dangerous mission. Whatever else she's done wrong, she's a very gutsy lady."

"She's very good to me."

"She's a bitch who humiliated me over and over. A bitch!"

Dave, "I understand."

To say that Dave was shocked when Mercedes asked if she could go with him and his wife to church one Sunday would be a vast understatement. "Why? You already go to your own church regularly. Are you dissatisfied?"

"No. I am quite happy in my church. But an old friend of mine, whom I admire more than I can say, has told me that I need to expand my understanding. This seemed like a good way. Also, I was hoping to meet your pastor, to understand why he thinks you should drop the case."

Maria intervened. "It is not our pastor's idea. It comes from the Lord. We do rely on him to help us feel the will of God. He is a good pastor. When we feel the will of God, it is our decision to obey."

"I didn't mean to offend you. But I have never felt the will of God like that. To tell me what to do. I have only felt his warmth, and guidance to do what is right."

"He deals with each of us differently. It is enough that you seek Him."

They took Mercedes to church that Sunday. It was like nothing that Mercedes had ever experienced before, filled with people, singing and dancing freely all over. *This is very strange. It is totally different from our church. I don't understand. I don't understand. What does it mean to them? It is clear they believe, and believe deeply. It makes no sense to me, but I must respect it. I am no better than them. They say they pray to the same God. They use Jesus' name as we do. But is it the same? I don't understand.*

After the service, Mercedes met the pastor. She thanked him for letting her come but admitted that it all felt very distant. "Why is it that we both pray to Jesus Christ, yet it feels so strange?"

"David and Maria told me that you are a good person. And so I do not doubt that you pray to our Lord. But I must say that many people say they pray to Jesus, but when I look at what they do, I know they do not. When I see evil, I know it comes from the devil. Those people say they follow our Lord, but in fact, they follow the devil."

"You believe in the devil?"

"You're asking if I believe that the devil is real and that he operates in our world? Of course, I do. I read my Bible. I know there is evil. And I know that the evil comes from the devil, I know there are a lot of so-called educated and modern people who don't believe in the devil, but they are wrong."

"Can't it be that the evil comes from within them? It comes from their lust, or greed, or whatever? How do you know it comes from the devil?"

"It doesn't come from nowhere. The evil is the devil acting in them."

"I do police work. I meet murderers, rapists, thieves, and a lot others who do evil, but they usually say they did not want to do evil."

"I believe them. But they are possessed by the devil, and in the possession of evil."

"Should we just forgive them? We can't punish the devil. What should we do?"

"You must punish them. Only the Lord gives forgiveness for sin. For some very personal sins, like adultery, the ones sinned against can give forgiveness. But otherwise, only the Lord."

"Why does the Lord not want Dave to help me find this murderer?"

"I don't know. All I do know is that we prayed together, and the spirit of the Lord entered us, and that was His will."

"Kitty can you please come in here."

"Certainly Mr. Rathbone. I'll be right there."

After the secretary walked into his office, he signaled for her to sit in one of the large comfortable chairs in the corner, and he sat down in one of the others. "As you know, the police are investigating the murder of Ted Alteman."

"Of course."

"Have you been interviewed?"

"No, I think I'm the only one who hasn't been. I don't think they've missed any secretary, but I guess they think a low-level clerk like me doesn't count."

"So they don't know…"

"No. I never told anybody what I saw and so there's no way for them to know."

"Good. And what will you do if they do interview you?"

"Exactly what do you mean?"

"Well, if they ask you do you know anything?"

"Do you mean will I offer them that I saw the two of you together?"

"Yes. They won't know to ask directly, but they could ask an open-ended question like, 'Do you know anything that we need to know?'"

"I'm not going to lie."

"I'm not asking you to lie. I'm asking if you will offer them information that they don't know to ask for?"

"I may be the only one who has seen you and Mrs. Alteman together, but I think every woman who works in this office understands what's been going on. Not just between you and Mrs. Alteman but also what was going on between Mr. Altman and Mrs. Neal. Any adult woman that's been alone with a man for 10 minutes could see what was happening."

"I'm sure you're right, but you are the only one who has what we call in the law business information of your own knowledge. That's different from just rumors."

"Mr. Rathbone, if you are asking me to lie or mislead the police, I won't do it. And I'm not a lawyer, but I know it's illegal to even ask me to. But you can be comfortable that I have no desire to hurt you."

I hope so.

Tyrone was in the kitchen. He yelled out, "The breakfast is ready."

"Give me a second to finish getting dressed and I'll be right there."

"Take your time."

She came into the kitchen, sat down, and took a sip of the coffee. "It's goodbye."

"What's goodbye?"

"I'm not coming back. We're over."

"Why? What happened?"

"I've wanted to end it for weeks now, even months. Trouble is you're too damn handsome, too smart, and too everything. Finally, I said, get one more good night in bed bite the bullet, and end the affair. So that's what I'm doing."

"Why?"

"I don't know what she did to you, but you're a wounded duck. You try to flap your wings, but you can't fly. It's that simple."

"Solly, I'm worried."

"Why?"

"The police came back. They had some crazy story about Ted taking me on extravagant trips to foreign countries. Sooner or later, they will realize that whoever he was traveling with was not me. But while they do that, sooner or later, they will realize that we've seen each other many times."

"I guess that will be embarrassing, but it's not a real problem."

"I think it is. They will think that you or I or both of us together, killed him so that we could be together."

"Well, God knows the motivation was there."

"If they can't find the killer, they will have no choice but to frame us."

"You're right. The police never admit failure."

As always, when Mercedes faced a hard problem, she went to the professor... even if now she was supposed to call him Krishna. "How do people have such absolute faith?"

The old man petted her almost as he might his beloved dog. He looked at her and smiled. "Ah yes, those are the ultimate questions. Those other questions no one can ever answer."

Mercedes sagged and smiled back.

"The keyword is absolute. You and I both have faith, but our faith is a little mushy. We get to explain what we can't understand by saying, simply 'I don't know'. They deal with the same problem with 'God works his wonders in mysterious ways'. I don't know how they do it either. I prefer our way, but I'm not sure how big the difference is really."

CHAPTER 26

THE TEST

The following evening, "I will give you some special food tonight at dinner. Afterward, we will go to a special room which is all dark. We will sit in separate chairs. I will say nothing, and I will do nothing. I will not touch you unless the experience is too much for you. If it is, I will turn on the lights and it will be over. Otherwise, it will be the moment of truth for your whole life."

"Did you drug me last night? You are scaring me."

"You will wear a loose dress with nothing on underneath."

"Why? Is this some kind of religious ritual?"

"No, but you could call it that. I will protect you if you need it. But if you do well, it will change your life forever, as it did me." He petted her hair and kissed her hand. "I like you a lot."

"I like you also. But I have children back home, and they must come first before anything." Later they went into the room.

Many voices, from many directions, sometimes overlapping, with many other sounds.

"Stand up."

"Don't move."

Linda, "I ..."

"Be silent. We will tell you when to speak."

"You're lying."

"Trust her."

"What is your name?"

"We don't need to ask her that. We all already know her name."

"We need to test her."

Linda, "Why? ..."

"Look at me."

Linda, "I don't know where to look."

"It doesn't matter, we are wherever you look."

"I trust her."

Linda, "Why am I here?"

"Because Pablito thinks you are suitable."

"No, because we let him get out of control."

"That's the real truth. It's our fault."

"It's your fault, not our fault. Our group never agreed."

"We don't need to argue about that now. It's been dealt with. We have to evaluate her."

Linda, "To evaluate me for what? Why am I here?"

"To be accepted."

Linda "To be accepted into what? I don't understand. I don't understand. What is happening to me?"

"Into a relationship with us, or at least some of us. We don't always agree."

"The first question is, will you be obedient?"

Linda, "No! I am not an obedient person. I do what I think is right, not what someone else tells me."

"You do not understand. And the problem now is that you do not understand that you do not understand. You are still caught by the limitations of being human. If you are allowed to join, you will transcend those limits."

Linda "Who are you?"

"Truth beyond understanding. Reality beyond light."

Linda, "Are you God?"

"It is a foolish question. You will misunderstand every possible answer. What is at issue is do you have the humility to obey without understanding?"

"If you thought we were God, would you obey?"

"Of course. I am a good person, and I would always wish to do as God would wish me to do."

"But God is beyond your understanding. You said that you were so willful that you would not obey what you do not understand."

"Well obviously God is different."

"You do have the humility to obey what you do not understand if, in some way, you come to understand the importance of that which you do not understand?"

"My head is swimming. What does it mean 'to understand the importance of that which you do not understand'."

"Get naked."

Linda, "I don't want to."

"Do as you're told or the session is over."

Linda, "I ... "

"Do as you are told or the session is over."

Linda undressed.

"Get on your knees."

Linda drops down to her knees.

"Be silent while we examine your soul."

Linda remained silent.

"You may get dressed. We are done."

Pablito stood up and turned on the light.

"Did you see what they did to me?"

"I saw nothing."

"Did you hear what they said to me?"

"I heard nothing."

"How did you know to turn on the light"

"I just felt that it was time. That's how it is."

"They said I was to be judged to see if I would be accepted."

"Of course, that was the whole point."

"And am I accepted?"

"I don't know. I will never know, but at some point, you will know."

"And how will I know?"

"You just will know. Your life will be changed."

"Does that mean I will have some special power?"

"I don't know. They do what they do for their reasons. But when you see it, when you feel it, when it happens, there is no question, but that it is them."

"What happens now?"

"That's up to you. If you choose to go home you can."

"I don't want to go home yet. Let me tell you something you don't know. The idea for someone to come here came from the San Francisco police. When my ex-husband refused, I volunteered. I have my reasons, but for them, I am supposed to find out who killed Ted. I have learned that Ted was a manipulative son of a bitch and deserved to die even more than I realized. I have learned that there are mysterious powers involved, which I do not understand, and which may play a role in my life in the future. But I have no idea who killed Ted, and that is what I promised to try to learn. I asked Angela and she was evasive."

"Are you asking me who killed him? I don't know. And to be honest, even if I did know, I probably would not tell you. That's not the way it works. I think you can know that they wanted him to die, and that, in some sense, they arranged it. That's not to say they told someone to do it. That's not how they work. But maybe you should ask Angela again now that you have been through the test."

"I still don't get it, who are they?"

"That's exactly right. They are a power that exists in the world, and that you do not, and will never understand, even if it plays a role in your life."

"OK, if I can't do anything about who they are, and you won't tell me who killed Ted, then what can I do to fulfill my promise to the San Francisco police?"

"I think you can understand that his murder was accomplished by many people who not only do not know each other but also did not know they were a part of a murder. You can know that even the murderer, and the other people who played a role in accomplishing the murder, do not now remember why they did what they did, or usually even that they did it. Much as you don't remember why you had the affair with Ted."

"Then, how am I ever going to make sense of the murder?"

"You can look around and see if there are pieces of the plot that you can find, each of which does not know that it was in the plot, but which you can put together in your mind and realize that is how the plot worked."

"I have no idea how to use that statement."

"Who told you to advertise in order to come here?"

"Frank Agri."

"What did he tell you?"

"He said it probably had something to do with the queen, and that if I wanted to talk to the queen, I had to come to you. So I did."

"The queen is simply street talk for things they do not understand. You could say it was their word for the power that you have now experienced. After Angela, I suggest you go back to Mr. Agri and ask him again what he knows. If they want you to know more, then he will give you a clue, and you will go with that."

"Don't try to put me off. You know more than I'll ever know and I'm here now. I want to know what you know."

He kissed her hand. "Good night." Then he turned and left.

CHAPTER 27

LOOSE ENDS

The mayor had been on the chief's back about this case from the beginning, but he had not involved himself in the details. Now the chief asked for and got a meeting with the mayor. He brought Mercedes. "If the Alteman murder wasn't big enough and weird enough already, now it appears to be also at least a major theft if not a financial scandal. There are millions of dollars, maybe tens of millions or more, missing from his accounts."

The mayor leaned forward. *This will be bigger headlines than the murder.* "How much money are we talking about?"

Mercedes said, "We can't be sure. He appears to have had many bank accounts, some of them Swiss or other secret locations. And the transactions that had been flowing through the ones we do know about are very strange. There are cash withdrawals of tens and hundreds of thousands of dollars in a single day, and often for days on end. We can be pretty sure that as recently as last year he was worth no less than $400 million. All we can find now is about $20 million in cash in banks and the value of his house at about $20 million or more. Someone said his wife's jewelry is also worth on the order of $10 million."

"So at least $400 million is missing, correct?"

"At a minimum."

"And we can't trace any of it?"

"Plus or minus a few million, that's right."

"At the risk of sounding stupid, how is that possible?"

"We don't know yet. About three months ago, the money stopped pouring into his accounts, but it's never stopped pouring out. He used to have balances totaling in the hundreds of thousands, but now they're all near zip. A large amount was taken out in cash on the day he died."

"There was no money on his body when he was found?"

Mercedes again, "Correct, but remember, he was not dressed in the clothes that he wore when he came in."

"So the killer knew he had the money on him. Was it a drug deal gone bad?"

"There is no evidence that he did drugs or trafficked in them."

"Then why did he have so much money on him?"

"We are pretty sure that the reason he was there was to meet his girlfriend, Sally, but then she backed out."

"Was she blackmailing him?"

"There's no evidence for that. And if she was, and if the money was to pay her blackmail, then why should she kill him? Or more accurately, have him killed, since we know, she was elsewhere with another man at the time he was killed."

Now the mayor was almost enjoying the mystery. "She conned him in some way so that he was bringing the money to her. She wanted the money but did not want to continue the con. Therefore, she arranged the murder, perhaps used some of the money to pay the killer, and had her money."

"That may be right, but it's just a theory. We don't even know where the money was on him. We don't know the killer. All we know is that she arranged and backed out of the assignation and that he withdrew a lot of money. I don't think you can even call that circumstantial evidence."

"You're right. We can't arrest her. But we need to check her out, including her bank accounts, very carefully."

"That's only the beginning of the problem. We don't know where his money came from. It's true he made a lot of money as a lawyer, but not that much. Not nearly that much. There is more to his life than we know."

"What could that be?"

"One possibility is Gulov. Perhaps he got the money either from Gulov for Russian political reasons, or because of his narco friends. Maybe Gulov took back the money. Maybe there was some big fight amongst them and that's why they're both dead."

"If it's anything like that, we'll never know."

Less than an hour later the chief and Mercedes were back in the mayor's office. "Now, in addition to murder and mega theft, we have an international angle. Apparently, Gulov went crazy before he died. He left a crazy recorded note that people were trying to kill him."

Mercedes, "And now he's dead. His private jet blew up in flight."

"We think it was not an airplane accident. We think someone set out to kill him."

The mayor was totally focused. "And how do *we* know the accident was not an accident?"

"What else could it be? Suicide?"

"He wasn't the suicidal type."

"Then what happened?"

The chief pulled out a mobile phone. "Listen to this."

I am being hunted like a stray dog. They will stop at nothing. Yesterday they tried to poison me, but I realized what they were doing, and threw it out. Before that, I was being followed and stalked by a killer. I could see the gun hidden under his jacket. I started to walk faster and faster and he followed me. But then I

*went into a restaurant and left through a window in
the toilet and he wasn't able to follow me, but the
bastard will be back. I am being hunted like a dog.
They will get me sooner or later.*

"That is crazy. What happened?"

"Is it possible that he did something to anger the queen, like
Ted? Is that the 'they'?"

"If we believe that, then we are starting to be as crazy as he was."

"That message doesn't sound like it was just an accident."

"No. I think that someone close to him, who is perhaps involved
in the murder of Ted, felt we were getting too close, and found a
way to protect himself, which was to get rid of the link, Gulov."

"Who?"

"One thing is he had a lot of connections back in Russia. When
they want to, they can play very rough. Maybe he crossed one of
them, but if that's the case, we'll never know. The other possibility
is that the studio had some backers who make their money and
drugs, etc. It might be one of them."

"Could it be El Sueño?"

"The word 'could' is a useless word. Anything could. We don't
know."

"Do you think it is El Sueño?"

"No, I don't. He sells drugs, but he stays away from murder. I
think it is either a Russian or one of the Latin American narcos who
were invested in the studio and other things that Gulov was
involved in."

Solly and Frank had almost nothing in common, but in some
ways, they were almost identical. Solly was hyper-respectable, while
Frank, despite the money and the middle-class upbringing, was
closer to his grandfather, a petty crook. Solly was older, shorter,

fatter, and with less hair. Nevertheless, they both lived by their wits and trusted nobody.

"It's true. He gambled a lot. So what?"

"You can be sure the police will be here asking the same questions that I want. Thank you for talking to me. The fact is that there are a few hundred million dollars missing."

"He's dead and it's not your money. So why do you care?"

"As I told you, I am the head of the firm he worked in. The police will be asking me also. And I am a friend of his wife, the widow. If possible, I would like to help her recover some of the money."

"I don't know anything about that kind of money. His bets with me were usually a few thousand dollars. Most of the payoffs were also a few thousand, or sometimes 10 or $20,000. I do remember one time he took a long shot in a horse race and I think he got something over $100,000. But I don't know anything about millions."

"I heard that you paid for the murder."

"That's not true. I did send about $30,000 to a guy I knew in San Francisco and now it seems that he had something to do with it. But I had nothing to do with it."

"They tell me that Ted may have had more than $100,000 on him when he was killed. Someone wanted that money."

"I don't know anything about that. I did get a mysterious package with $40,000 in cash in it the day after he was murdered. I have no idea where it came from."

The two men just looked at each other and it was over.

I don't like it. I'm back to being an ordinary cop. But there's so much pressure on this case, and with Dave wanting to drop out and doing only the minimum, there's nothing else I can do. "Ms. Harris, I have a search warrant."

"You have what?"

"We have a search warrant to go through the house and the outside buildings. Mr. Alteman had a great deal of money on him when he was murdered. You arranged for him to be in the place where he was murdered. We think you set him up to get the money."

"That's crazy! I don't need his money."

"We have a warrant."

"Let me see it."

Sally examined the warrant. "You can look anywhere you want."

Mercedes waved them forward. Johnny and three other men spread out through the house. "We will try to be respectful, but we must look everywhere. We have to look in your personal files and in your underwear drawer."

"I understand. Look wherever you want."

As Mercedes was getting dressed in the morning, she looked in the mirror, and she suddenly had one overwhelming thought. *Do it now! Make the change! It's your life, now or never!* She just stood there for a long moment. *What's wrong? I don't understand. They all say I'm good-looking, even beautiful. God knows enough men are trying. And they're not bad men, but I don't want them. I want to have a family. I want children, even a lot of them. It's not that. I still have time. I certainly have a good job. I make enough money and I'm getting promoted. Soon I'll be making a lot more. I don't understand. That's the real problem, that I don't understand. More than anything I want a meaningful life. Too many lives are just empty. Filled with games, money, sex, whatever, but not any meaning. It's good to get the extra education but I don't find the meaning. The professor knows the meaning, but he can't give it to me. He tries and I try to learn, and I'm not stupid, but it doesn't happen. Sometimes I think the only meaning is family. That's why the lives of my parents and other uneducated people are as meaningful as anybody else. But it doesn't happen to me.*

I need to do it now! I don't know what it is but whatever it is I need to do it now. Make the change! I need to do it now!

CHAPTER 28

PABLITO

"When do I leave?"

"Tomorrow, if you want."

"How do I leave?"

"Pretty much the way you came. You will go to sleep here, and wake up there."

"How do I thank you? It all feels crazy, but I do feel I know how Ted died, what happened to me, and perhaps even who I am."

"You have no reason to thank me. I had nothing to do with it."

"I am conflicted. I can't stay. I have children and a life that I need to go back to. But you are a very charming man. And I do want to stay for you."

"We'll take it one day at a time. We can talk about it again tomorrow." They spent the night together.

Pablito and Linda went on the same walk they had taken on her first day in Chiapas.

"I need to understand the mystery. Is this force you talk about just another word for God?"

"What do you think God is? An old man sitting in heaven, taking reports on teenagers, or married women having affairs?"

"I don't know. I'm not religious."

"That's a very good place to start. We all know that there are things that we do not understand. Some people take those things they don't understand and organize them into a set of ideas. Some of those ideas are very good and profound, so we call them religion. But some of them, I think, at least, are not just worthless, not just misleading, but bad. I think, instead, one should be humble, and simply admit that there is more to the world than we understand."

"You already got me to bed. You don't need to feed me a lot of highfalutin crap."

"I'm not trying to feed you crap. You know I'm the big man in this little empire. I can have almost any woman I want, anytime I want."

"Do they want you?"

"To be honest, I don't know if they want to be with me or not. In general, I don't ask but they have no reason to be afraid of me. I would like to think that you wanted to be with me, and didn't just do it out of fear."

"I didn't do it out of fear. But if you don't care how I feel, it's the last time you'll touch me."

"I'm not callous. And I do care that if you go to bed with me, you do it because you want to."

"Let's get back to your God."

"As I said, I don't believe in God. But I am humble before the reality of power I don't understand. And I have come to understand that if you are humble toward that power, it can and will intervene in your life in ways that you cannot imagine any other way."

"Your God answered your prayers?"

"Not at all. I don't pray and if I did, I would not ask for anything specific, because I know that's not how it works. For better or worse, whether I wanted it or not, things happen, both inside my head and in the world, in which I feel the power. I think it's clear that the death of your lover was such an event. I feel that your experience here has changed you. That you have opened your mind to all the truth and force that is beyond understanding. When I learned that, I felt changed, and I still feel the change."

Linda was careful to think before she answered. *I think I have been initiated into the circle of the queen.* "I do feel different."

"Most people spend most or all of their lives focused on the things they understand, the few things they hope to learn. There's nothing wrong with that. They are good people and they are doing their very best. But once you have understood that almost everything that is true is beyond your understanding, then you turn your focus to the vast world of truth that you will never understand. You must learn to say things, and do things, and respond to feelings that make no sense. It is very disorienting. It is exhilarating to realize that you are in contact with truth beyond your understanding, and beyond the imagination of most of the people around you. But it is also crazy. Because you do not understand, you cannot tell moral from immoral, and truth from falsity. I suspect that's what happened to Ted. He let his narcissistic side come to the fore. From the limitations of all human beings, the ridiculous and the sublime look identical."

"It sounds like you're saying the queen runs your life. Or at the very least, she has so much control over your mind, that she could run your life if she wanted. It sounds like you are absolving people of all responsibility for what they do. Ted has no responsibility for seducing me and I have no responsibility for letting him."

"No, almost the opposite. We are all totally responsible for what we do. They can put ideas in our head, and then we can accept them or reject them. We have the choice."

"Then where is their power?"

"In my experience in my life, virtually everything I think to do comes from within me. Very rarely, I get ideas that seem to come out of nowhere. And I do mean rarely. But I have gotten in the habit of treating those rare thoughts with special respect. That respect comes from the times when thoughts like those changed my life. Sometimes the thoughts are just about me or incidentals in my life. But sometimes, those thoughts seem to be part of an unseen truth outside of me. When I decided to resist the Mexican army, I had no reason to believe I would survive. But when the miracle occurred that they defeated themselves, and then left us alone, I learned to treat those thoughts with great respect and love."

"So perhaps that can explain why you chose to resist the Mexican army, but it does not explain what happened to the Mexican army."

"I don't know. I don't know. But I imagine that they flooded each of the soldiers, or at least many of them, with thoughts that one of the other soldiers was trying to shoot them either out of malice or confusion. And then the confusion turned into chaos, and they defeated themselves."

"Was the Mexican army, so confused as to be defenseless."

"That's not the way I would see it. The soldiers of the Mexican army had good reasons to be unmotivated and suspicious of each other. It didn't take much to incite the confusion. You can't blame them for your decision to have an affair. The most you can say is they encouraged you. Or perhaps you didn't need any encouragement, you wanted it all by yourself."

As they walked further, they started to hold hands.

Then, at a point where there was a beautiful view over the valley, Pablito took her in his arms and gave her a deep kiss.

"Angela and the women asked if they could make you a farewell banquet. I hope you don't mind but I said yes."

"Of course. I'm honored but I have done nothing to deserve it."

"We have all enjoyed your visit."

"You've made me happy also."

"Do you like music?"

"Yes. What type do you like?"

"Everything, and you?"

"Perhaps not everything, but I do have a varied taste. Did you have something you wanted to share?"

"Yes." He led her into the living room, settled her in a warm chair, and went to play on the piano and sing, not that he had a good voice. "It is a French love song from before the revolution called Plasier d'amour, the pleasure of love. The line that is repeated is, 'The joy of love is but a moment long. The pain of love endures the whole life long.'"

"It's so beautiful and so true."

"Can you stay with me?"

"Tonight?"

"If not for the rest of our lives, then for a while. You are beautiful, smart, and brave. I'm in love as I have never been before."

"You are strong, handsome, sweet, and more than a little bit lonely. What more could any woman ask?"

"Then you will stay?"

"No. I have debts to pay and promises to keep. Debts to my ex-husband and promises to my children. I could love you. It breaks my heart, but I leave tomorrow without fail."

"Perhaps afterward you will come back."

"If I can, I surely will."

CHAPTER 29

RETURN

Linda went into the kitchen. "Can I help?"

"Thank you, but you are the guest of honor. It would not be appropriate."

"It would be an honor to me to learn some of the tricks of Mexican cooking."

"There are no tricks. It's peasant food. It is a lot of work."

"Please let me do something. I would enjoy feeling the connection."

Angela started to laugh. "OK, you can chop lettuce."

"Where is there an apron I can wear?"

"Over there in the corner."

Linda went and put on the apron and started to chop lettuce. "Can I ask you something personal?"

"You can ask."

"I sense you're a very strong woman. Why do you accept the subordinate position?"

"Why do you think I'm subordinate?"

"Pablito is in charge here. Aren't you subordinate to him?"

"I don't see it that way. He has his role and I have mine."

"But in the end, men always want to be the boss?"

"That's their problem. If they step over the bounds, then you have to remind them."

"Some try to use force to get their way. What do you do then?"

"Sometimes you have to use force to remind them."

"Like what?"

"Years ago I had a boyfriend who thought he could be rough with me. I told him to stop and he didn't. He was selling drugs, and maybe he started taking more of his own stuff than he should have. One time when he came over, I drew a gun on him and walked him to the police station. I told him and the police to arrest him for his own protection. I told him if I ever saw him again, they would find him dead."

"Would you really have killed him if he came over again?"

"I mean what I say."

"You are the most radical feminist I ever met."

"I don't know much about feminism, that's not a part of this world. But from what I can see it's all nonsense. It's just a lot of high-class women wanting to make a scene."

"They just want to be treated as equals. They want to be treated fairly."

"It's a world I don't know. Perhaps it's necessary there."

"Don't you ever get harassed by men trying to hit up on you? A lot of the men I've seen around here look pretty tough."

"They try, and if I want to I do, and if I don't want to, I don't."

"But don't they harass you? Keep trying in aggressive ways?"

"If I tell them to get lost, they stay away."

"That doesn't work for many women. The men keep trying, no matter what you do."

"I don't believe that. If you have to, you just threaten to cut it off."

"I finished the lettuce. What else should I do?"

"Chop these tomatoes."

"Don't you feel stifled in this environment? You're such an amazing woman. You're smart, good-looking, and with a power inside like no one I've ever seen. Don't you feel crushed to be here?"

"I'm happy."

"Don't you have dreams?"

"I have wonderful dreams. Every night in my dreams, I go to my second life and it is so beautiful."

"You have dreams that make sense when you wake up in the morning?"

"In my dreams, I live in a world beyond the stars, beyond the light, and beyond any human understanding. I go there every night."

"You take drugs?"

"Of course not. We sell drugs, but I feel sorry for the fools who take them. They prefer those delusions to reality."

"And the second life you have, beyond the stars, you call that reality?"

"Of course. What else is it?"

"They're dreams. They're not real. They are just some figments of your imagination when you were asleep."

"I don't see why they are any less real than what I see when I'm awake."

"Because they're dreams. Nobody thinks that dreams are real."

"I don't care what you or anybody else thinks. They are my dreams. They are the world I live in when I'm asleep in this world."

"Are you the same person in that other world that you are here?"

"It's a very different world. You don't have a body there. And they don't have things like kitchens, or houses, etc. but there are people with personalities. There are colors and sounds. There are feelings of joy and sadness. It's not always wonderful there, but I do like it."

"Angela, please, I beg you, don't make fun of me. This is very important to me. Are you serious?"

"Why would you even imagine that I am making fun of you? I'm simply telling you my experience. If your experience is different, so be it. If I were in your situation and had someone explain to me some things that they had experienced and I had not, I would want to learn and understand what they have experienced. I would treat it as my ignorance, not as their error, or failing."

What do I do with that? She's not crazy. She's quite smart and stable. No one treats the dream world as real.

After that, Linda chopped some onions, and then her time in the kitchen was over.

"I think the chief needs to hear this direct. I have a guy on the phone from Folsom prison. He says that he had dealt with Ted Alteman, and he has a story to tell."

"Give me a second and I'll put him on."

"This is the chief. What do you want?"

"Sir, my name is Jimmy Johnson and I am in Folsom prison. I was convicted of a murder that I had nothing to do with. Your dead man framed me."

"Listen, Mr. Johnson, every prisoner says he was innocent and half of them say they were framed. Please don't waste my time."

"Sir, if you remember the case, I said that I was framed at the time of the trial by a man I had never met before. When I saw the face in the newspaper of your dead man, I recognized it immediately. I beg you, to listen to me. I don't want to die in prison. I was a pimp and I ran six girls. That guy used two or three of them a few times. He came up to me and acted like my friend after he was done with one of them. He offered to buy me a drink and like an idiot I let him do it. While we were having the drinks, he showed me the gun he had bought and handed it to me to look at. That's how it got my fingerprints. That's the only thing that connected me to the murder that I was convicted of. I'm innocent. I swear I am innocent."

"I want to get back to work. I'll look into it. I'm busy now. Goodbye."

"Linda here again. I'm coming home tomorrow. Well to be exact, I'm leaving here tomorrow. It took four days to get here, so I don't know when I'll be back in fact."

"Well, I'm glad of that. Do you now understand the case?"

"I think I understand important parts and I think I understand that there are some parts that will never be clear. But I do think we can put it all together as a story that makes some sense. This has been the most amazing experience of my life."

"At one point I was worried you were going to fall in love with him and stay there."

"I would say he as much as proposed, but I told him no. My children come first, always. And besides, although he is very charming, and I certainly could learn to love him, I'm in love with Tyrone, no matter how much he hates me."

Mercedes finished making dinner for her parents. "I am going away for a while. I'm not sure exactly when I'll be back."

Mama could see that she meant more than she said. "You're going on a vacation?"

"I don't know. I don't know what to expect at all, but I have to try to find a new way. My life's not going in the way I want it to."

Papa looked at her. "It's not a part of your job?"

"No. I'm quitting my job."

Mama, "Why, baby? It's a great job and you've gotten promoted."

"I know. But something keeps telling me in my head, that I have to make a change. I have to make a big change to put my life in the right direction."

Fog, envelop me I beg you.
Fog, blessed fog, carry me.
Fog, home to joy and pain.
Fog, home, past and future.

Fog, the comfort of dreams.
Fog, the anguish of regret.
Fog, my lost innocence.
Fog, leading to fog leading to fog ...

PART III
ALL'S WELL

CHAPTER 30

START AGAIN

Linda woke up very slowly in her bed in her home. It was the middle of the night, the room was dark, and she was completely disoriented. For just a moment, she was so frightened as to think she was dead. But as she moved around and touched things, she recognized her bedside table and other familiar objects. She got up and turned on the lights. She was dressed in the same gown that she had been wearing when she was first kidnapped. She smiled and realized what good care they had taken of her. She closed her eyes and kissed Pablito on the lips in her mind.

What am I going to do with the rest of my life? I accept responsibility for what I have done. I can't lose focus on the core fact. I destroyed my life with a lie. But that is history now. I am a mother, with no right to die. Still, I will not ... I cannot live without joy and hope. Where do I find the strength? My children are my road to redemption. How? I am filled with confusion. I'm not embarrassed by my desires and lust. Yet my wish to be good must come first. Even now, I've been on this road too long. I need to be strong. I swear I will fight to the finish. What if this last voyage was all a dream? Can my life be salvaged with a new man? Maybe, but first I must try for Tyrone. I want Tyrone. I will pay my debts. Most essential to have a chance is courage. A future worth having is filled with risk.

The mayor called the kind of meeting that he never calls. "I called this meeting because I have to get a grip on the Alteman murder case. There are a lot of people interested in what happened to Ted Alteman. They are more interested because so much time is dragged on and because everything that's leaked out has spoken of some kind of weird conspiracy. This has to stop. I met Ted Alteman more than a few times. I know all about his amazing courtroom cases and the stories of all women. You know the news as well as I do, and the rumors are getting more and more salacious. This has to stop."

The chief was in a foul mood. "The mayor has been very open and fair with me in this matter. I have no complaints. But I'm getting the shit beat out of me because of this case. I told you from the start, and I certainly don't need to tell you now, that the press on the public want it solved and solved promptly. Instead, it's dragged on with no arrests. Starting now this case is going to move to an arrest."

Mercedes begged Dave to come, and he did, very reluctantly. Dave brought Johnny.

Dave, "The first obvious suspect is his wife. She had plenty of motive. He cheated on her with more women than I can count. She lied to us. She said she didn't have a boyfriend and we now know that she did and still does. No one would've had it easier, either to get him to go to the hotel, or follow him to the hotel and then to be admitted into the room with no resistance. The gun he was killed with is a woman's gun. And now she's free to enjoy her boyfriend. You can't make a better murder suspect than that."

The chief then almost leaped out of his chair. "Then go arrest her and bring her in."

Mercedes, "But we know she is not the person who got him set up to go there. It was the cowgirl, Sally Harris. And she has no connection to Frank Agri, who's the guy that put the plot in motion."

The chief's voice sounded desperate. "Maybe she colluded with Harris. She threatened to make a scandal and harassed her to help."

As much as I admire him, he's ready to frame my mother to get this case closed. Mercedes, "I don't think that Harris could be manipulated that easily."

"One way or the other, the wife is a prime suspect."

"She has no alibi. Why is she not the suspect, and under arrest?"

"Chief, if you saw her, you wouldn't think it was her. She just doesn't look the type."

"None of them look the type. I want you to go there and either she has an alibi, or bring her in under arrest."

He may be desperate, but arresting her will get us laughed out of town. Mercedes, "I think it might be Solomon Rathbone, the head of the law firm, and the wife's boyfriend, and almost certainly her lover. He lied to us about that. But I think the biggest thing is at the end, to know Ted Alteman was to hate him, and that's how Rathbone felt. I think if the wife played a role, it was to goad Rathbone. Something like, 'If you love me, set me free and get rid of him.'"

Dave, "I don't believe it. Neither of them are the killer type. They're more likely to be afraid of blood than to commit murder."

"People say that about every middle-class killer. It's nothing but class prejudice."

"There are too many ifs to make him a prime suspect. We don't have real proof of how close he was to the wife, and we don't have real proof about how much he hated the dead man, and we don't have any other motive. It was a woman, given the murder weapon."

"Does he have an alibi?"

Johnny, "I don't think we've ever asked him directly."

"Then haul him in, sweat him, and demand an alibi. And if he doesn't have an alibi, or the only one he has is dependent upon the widow, arrest him as an accessory."

Dave started to get worked up. "He has no connection to the cowgirl. If you don't explain Sally Harris, and why she set him up, then you'll have nothing."

There was a long, uncomfortable silence. The chief leaned back in his chair and covered his face with his hands. "What do you want me to do?"

Mercedes, "There are plenty of other reasonable suspects. I don't believe it, but what about Tyrone Neal? He's a tough guy from a tough background and his hate for Alteman drips out of every sentence. He has a weak alibi. He says he went to the mountains, but there's no solid corroboration."

Dave, "Why, if he was the murderer, does he go out of his way always to tell us how motivated he was? Wouldn't he hide it?"

Mercedes, "Maybe it's a judo move. He makes it clear he was motivated, so we ask just that question and therefore don't take him seriously as a suspect."

The chief, "How good is his alibi?"

"I don't remember exactly, but he says he did stop at a café, where people know him, and he may have bought gas."

"Let's check those out. And if they don't check out, bring him in too."

"I don't think you should leave out the former Mrs. Neal. She is a tough lady and Alteman dumped her hard, very hard."

Mercedes, "She's working with us now to try to figure out what's going on."

Now it was the mayor's term to get riled up. "I've been told she's trying to sell this cock-and-bull story about the mysterious force called the queen. It sounds like bullshit to me and we shouldn't buy it for a second."

Dave, "I'll tell you again, if you don't explain Sally Harris, and why she set him up, then you have nothing."

Johnny, "While you're on the topic of Linda Neal, there is her live-in boyfriend. He's not a sweetie pie. He has half a dozen arrests for drunkenness and brawling and even a few months for manslaughter. Maybe she told him to pay the rent, or get even for her."

"Well, he could not have gotten him into the hotel. She would've had to do that."

"Fair enough."

"Chief, she's working for us now. It makes no sense."

One woman trying to protect another. "That counts for nothing. If she was guilty, it'd be a great way to cover it up."

"But we know that the woman who got him there was not her, but Sally Harris. There's simply nothing to connect her."

"OK. Keep her on the back burner for now."

"The problem is that we're not done. There are other good suspects. We can go back to Sally Harris herself. We know she's the one who set him up. And the guy she was supposed to be with, her alibi, is not rock solid. He could be doing it as a favor to her. We don't know."

"Have you spoken to the guy she said she was with?"

"No, she said he's married, and we didn't want to cause more trouble than we had to."

"Pull the son of a bitch in and ask him. I don't care if he brings his wife with him."

"Chief, do we have to…"

"I said do it!"

"And there's a husband of the doctor down in Monterey, who did threaten to kill him."

"They say they were together that night at home."

"OK, keep them on the back burner."

"And last, but not least, are Gulov and friends. He may be dead. I know that he or one of the other people who lost $1 billion are just the type to have done the murder, or more accurately to have the murder done by someone else."

"That should include Frank Agri. He's not a partner with Gulov, but he's involved in that kind of stuff. And then there's the question of the money. There's the big money that disappeared, and the craziness that Frank was reimbursed for his expenses, we don't know how, and with a $10,000 tip."

"And we got this off-the-wall call about a guy in Israel. We haven't followed that up."

"I think Gulov and the Israeli are too far afield just now. Let's talk to Agri one more time."

"And then there is the 800-pound gorilla in the room. The idea is that there is a mastermind behind the murder, not any of the reasonable suspects. The person, the organization, the myth that they call the queen. It's too crazy to consider, but there are crazy facts that don't fit any reasonable suspect. Why did Frank Agri pay for the gun? Who arranged to place the gun for the murder? Who paid the hooker to turn off the surveillance cameras? None of the suspects fit into that story, but they are facts of the story. We know the murder weapon but we don't know the murderer or the person who organized the plot."

"There is no way to sell that crazy story to the public, not to mention all the big shots. They keep asking for an answer."

"I agree. But the problem is, it's the only answer that comes close to the facts."

"I'm not going in front of the cameras, or in front of the big shots, and try to pedal a crazy story like that. I'd look like an idiot."

Mercedes met Linda for lunch at a beautiful restaurant with a view of the bay. They greeted each other as old friends, even though in fact, they hardly knew each other. They felt the bond between them, but they had no idea just how bonded they were.

"Let's do the police stuff first. Do you know who did it?"

"I can't be sure. No one ever admitted anything. But they didn't deny it either. Pablito doesn't leave the mountain, so it wasn't him.

If you make me guess, I think it was Angela. It could've been one of the other women that I didn't get to know as well, but Angela is the most important woman. For something big like this, I think they would send her."

"Who is they? Pablito?"

"Again, I don't know, but I don't think so. There's something mysterious about the way they work. They seem to be coordinated, but not by talking to each other. Certainly not by giving orders. It's as if they could read each other's minds. I know it sounds crazy, but it's the best I can do."

"What do they say? How do they say they get along?"

"They don't. In some ways, it's almost like that comedy routine, where each comedian responds to the other's previous sentence before the first one has finished his sentence."

"Pablito is the boss?"

"Yes. He says he is, and they all say he is, but then they all agree he doesn't tell them what to do. I don't know how that works."

"What about Angela?"

"In some ways, she's both very impressive and very nice. But she said some things that are just crazy. She said she lives in a whole separate world when she's asleep and that world is just as real as this world is. That's crazy."

"That is crazy. Does she act crazy?"

"Not at all. She told me the craziness while we were chopping food in the kitchen. She's not crazy at all."

Mercedes leaned back and just stared at Linda's eyes. Linda stared back. It was a long silence but neither looked away. Then, finally, Linda looked away and said, "What do you want to know?"

"Whatever you want to tell me."

"What if I don't want to tell you anything?"

"I can't make you. But I think we've become friends, and I'm hoping you'll tell me everything."

"I came back home, didn't I? Doesn't that say everything?"

"No. It doesn't say anything about what happened."

"The only thing that matters is I came home to my children."

"I agree that's the big thing, but not everything."

"What do you want to know?"

"What was it like?"

"To the day I die, it will be the most exciting thing I ever did."

"How so?"

"It was a trip to the Mountain top and back."

"What did you find at the top of the mountain?"

"A group of Mexicans, living together in a kind of commune, working together, appearing very happy."

"And you wanted to stay?"

"Yes, but no. I am a mother and my children come before anything and everything."

"But if not for your children you wanted to stay?"

"Absolutely!"

"What about Tyrone?"

"I want him too. I wish I could have both."

The rest of the lunch was just lighthearted girl talk.

CHAPTER 31

I WANT ...

"I know you both met once before when I decided to quit the case, but Captain Mercedes asked to come and talk to us again. So I brought her here today."

"Thank you, Pastor, for taking the time to meet with me again today. I'm trying to understand something, which is very hard for me and which I believe you can help me with."

"That's what I do in the service of the Lord. I will do my best."

"I was born and raised Catholic, and I go to church regularly. When I asked my priest this question, I was not satisfied with his answer. I don't want you to think that I am about to leave my church. I am not, but I am interested in hearing your approach to this question. What do you mean when you speak of the devil?"

"I mean the devil. What else is there to say? The devil is the devil."

"Have you ever seen the devil?"

"No, of course not. The devil is not an animal that walks on earth. The devil is the spirit of evil that roams in the universe."

"Have you ever experienced the devil?"

"Of course. I think everyone has. I am blessed that when he tried to manipulate me, the Lord intervened and protected me."

"What does that mean, that the devil tried to manipulate you?"

"I felt myself being tempted, pushed or led toward evil. I may be a pastor, but I am a mortal flawed human being. Just like you."

"I don't get it."

"Surely you do. Is your life so pure, that you never wanted to do something wrong?"

"Of course not. Like anyone I have been tempted, but I decided not to."

"There is the difference. You have this pride that is so common today. Do you think that you are all powerful and can do whatever you want, uninfluenced by other things? You are wrong. The spirit of the Lord and the spirit of the devil are everywhere."

"I have never felt that."

"That is your lack of faith, your lack of wisdom. There was a time when people said they knew the sun goes around the Earth because they could see it moving across the sky around the Earth. But now we say the earth goes around the sun. We have a different understanding. I would say we have a different faith. We all see with the eyes of faith. Some people indeed think that their eyes of faith, that they call science, knows everything, and therefore anything it does not recognize does not exist. There's none so blind as them that will not see. If they could only have the humility of saying that their faith does not include all the things in the universe, then they too could learn to see the devil, and more importantly, the Lord."

"What does that humility entail?"

"Only that you open your mind to the idea that there are things you do not understand, probably never will understand, and perhaps you can never understand. First comes the humility. Once you have the humility, then you can look at the things you don't understand, particularly things that stand out like great virtue, and great evil, and ask yourself, where does that come from? What does it mean?"

"I feel I have that humility. I know that I and even all of science don't know everything. But I don't see the devil, or even the Lord, in my daily life."

"Then pray. And if you open your heart, the Lord will enter, and then all will be made, at least as clear as it can be to a mortal human being."

"God knows that's what I want."

"Chief, I want you to meet Ms. Linda Neal, the lady who went to see El Sueño in Chiapas."

"I must say Ms. Neal, you are a very brave woman. You could've been killed."

"Thank you for the compliment, chief, but I must say that everything I saw there was very different from what I imagined, and what I imagine you think. Let's start with the fact, that, as he wishes, I called him Pablito."

"Are you his friend?"

"Absolutely! He's a very nice man."

"He's a known killer and drug dealer. You call that a nice man?"

"He has admitted to me that he has killed people. He has admitted to me that they are involved in the drug trade. But he explained the murders in the context of people who wanted to kill him or people close to him. He explained the drugs as sold to people who wanted them, none of whom were forced to buy the drugs. I know that what he does is illegal. But he's still a very charming man. He treated me very well while I was there and returned me safely and unharmed. And I have to say, I believe that if I knew all the details of his crimes, it would not change the fact that I like him and think he's a good person."

"Then how can I trust what you tell me?"

"You can trust it as the truth of my experience while I was there. What you do with it is your responsibility."

"OK, I'll listen."

"I went to see him because we were told that he knew this mysterious entity, the queen, and that it, or she, or whatever ... was probably responsible for the murder of Ted Alteman, my former lover. Whatever the queen is, it's very hard to understand. As I understand it from Pablito, the queen is not a single entity, but rather multiple, which may not have much to do with each other. They are not people on earth or organizations or anything else that I have ever heard of. They are forces beyond understanding. But they are capable of putting ideas in peoples' heads that make them do things that they would not otherwise do, and also capable of making them forget what they did."

"Are they gods?"

"Maybe. I don't know. I only know what he told me."

"And did they order the murder?"

"I don't know how to answer that. I think the answer is closer to yes than to no, but the word order doesn't seem to fit."

"Then what happened?"

"Don't get me wrong. I'm pretty sure they had him killed. Someone pulled the trigger on a gun and the bullet killed him. I'm sure that in some sense they arranged for the killer to do that. But I don't think that a person was wide awake and received an explicit order to kill him. They just put ideas in their head and then probably had them forget it afterward."

"We have a picture of a woman we think might have been the killer. It's surveillance pictures of a woman who came from Guatemala City just before the murder and returned right afterward. Look at it."

Linda looks at the pictures. "I don't recognize the woman. I don't think it's Angela, the woman who's closest to Pablito on the mountaintop. But it could be her or one of the others. That's probably what they would do."

"Do you have any idea who it could be?"

"No. Pablito is a very intelligent man, and if he ordered it, he would surely send the woman in disguise. But I don't think he ordered it. Maybe it is Angela, just in disguise. I get the feeling that the way the queen, or whatever you want to call those mysterious powers, works is to put ideas in the mind of each person separately. Therefore, each person knows only what they need to know, and never sees the whole picture. But from experience, they sense they are being coordinated. So when they see something they did not expect, they ask themselves how it might fit into a larger plan. I don't know, but I imagine they told Pablito that they had something big to do so that he would not be surprised. They probably did not tell him anymore. And even calling it telling him, is misleading. I think all he got was a strong, but vague feeling. Therefore, when one of the women disappeared unexpectedly for some time, he understood."

"That won't work for the killer. She had to have rather explicit orders."

"From what I gather, she got those orders in separate parts. First to go to Guatemala City. Then take the airplane. Then to get the gun and shoot him. And then to go home. I expect that if you met her while she was doing this, you would find her a little bit in a fog. And afterward, she would not remember clearly any part of it."

"I have to tell you, this is very hard to believe. It's all magic and no one is responsible. I can't believe that."

"Neither would I before I went. But my experience there has changed me. Maybe it's the drugs they gave me. Maybe it's just because Pablito is very persuasive. I don't know. But I have a sense of humility before incomprehensible things, that I never had before. That's all I can say."

"What else do you know?"

"Nothing. ... Actually, that's not right. I do know something. I know something very profound, but I don't know how to say it. It is a feeling, not an idea. And it isn't even a feeling, like pain, or love, or hunger. It's more like a different consciousness. I know I am transformed. I just feel as if, not that I'm a different person, but that something deep in my nature has changed. My body hasn't changed. I have not learned anything new or forgotten anything old. I don't have a feeling of elation or sadness or anything like that. It is just that I have touched some deep meaning and I will never be the same."

"That's the way religious people talk."

"I don't feel religious, but I don't know what else to say."

Mercedes called Dave and asked him to come to her office. She explained her idea and asked for his help. "It's the right thing to do. I don't think I've ever said this before to anyone, but it's God's work." Dave consulted his wife and then agreed.

After they reminded Tyrone who they were, he let Mercedes and Dave into his living room.

"We are here on a strictly personal basis. The police force and the chief don't know. You might be able to get us fired for this, but we both thought it was important."

"You don't have to say a word. Just listen to us, and then we will leave."

"I want to talk to you as a woman who has become friends with your ex-wife"

"I want to talk to you as a man, whose heart was ripped up and spat on by a cheating woman."

Tyrone started to tear up, but with effort, he kept his composure.

"She was very brave to go to Mexico. She put herself in the hands of killers. As it turned out, she was not in danger. They had no reason to hurt her. But that doesn't change how brave she was."

"She was a great help to us. The murder of Mr. Alteman is the strangest case any of us have ever experienced, including the chief. But the key point is, she did not go to help us. She went because she feels guilty for what she did to you. She wanted to understand why she did something so terrible."

"I want to tell you two things out of my life. The first is that I almost killed myself with my anger and my pain at what she had done to me. Maybe you're just tougher than I am, but I want to warn you not to let it kill you. But the bigger thing is how my second wife saved my life. She took me to church and led me to give my life to Christ. I'm not telling you to become a Christian like we are. I am telling you that what I learned is that we are all sinners, and we all need forgiveness. Your ex-wife needs forgiveness and I believe, you would benefit if you forgive her."

Tyrone said nothing.

"Do you go to church?"

"No, not since I left to go to college. It may do something for you, but it's nothing to me now."

"You should give it a try."

Tyrone said nothing, and they left. He did not go to church. But a couple of days later, before he went to sleep, he did as he had been taught to as a child. He knelt down next to his bed and clasped his together. And then he cried for the first time as an adult.

CHAPTER 32

WOMEN

"Dr. Moore, how long did your affair with the murdered man, Ted Alteman, last?"

"About six months. My husband got a huge contract in Nevada, and so he was away a lot. And there was a big-time deadline, so he had to stay there, often even on weekends, to keep the crews going seven days a week. It made it all too easy."

"And how often did you see Ted?"

"Sometimes twice a week. Also, about three or four times we went away for a couple of days on vacation to Mexico."

"And you kept even those trips secret from your husband?"

"You may not believe this, but Ted had fake passports for himself and me every time. And they weren't the same name any two times in a row."

"And how did he describe you, this woman traveling with him?"

"When he took me places, he told them I was his wife. That's what the passports said. It was very good from my point of view."

"Did you enjoy the affair?"

"Of course. Why else would I do it?"

"I don't know. People do things for lots of reasons."

"He was the best lover I ever had. He was very attentive and very virile. What more could a girl ask?"

"Did you like him?"

"That's another question. He was always very nice to me. I would've dropped him in a second if he wasn't. But he didn't seem like a nice man. He was quite cruel to waiters, bell boys, and other people he looked down on."

"Did that bother you?"

"I think so. A little bit. But I didn't need him. I didn't need his money and perhaps besides my looks and whatever else, he liked the fact that he knew I could be tough if I wanted to."

The Chief yelled at his secretary, "All hands on deck! Cancel all leaves! I want all the commanders and detectives in my office within the hour!"

"It's a massacre?"

"Unbelievable. She killed 13 people."

An officer rushed in, "The number is now up to 24."

"And it's a woman? Women don't commit mass murders. I don't get it."

"No one gets it. It is crazy."

"I just can't imagine how it can happen. I can't imagine why it would happen."

"She was apparently perfectly normal. There's no history of mental illness. She just walked out of the house one day and bought a machine gun and two belts of bullets. Then she walked into the school and shot everyone she encountered. It's crazy."

"There has to be a reason. There has to be a reason. Maybe political. Something like that just can't come out of nowhere."

"So far they've turned up nothing."

CHAPTER 33

TOO BIG

Linda rang the doorbell. "I'm here to pick up the kids."

"I'll get them."

"Can I come in?"

"I'd rather you didn't. Every time I see you, a little more of me dies."

"Tyrone, I'm so sorry. I know it's all my fault. Please… "

"Please, don't start that again. I know who you are, and what you are. I'll get the kids, but I'd rather not talk to you."

"Tyrone, I'm begging."

"Go beg somewhere else."

When he came back Linda reached out to take his hand, but he would not let her, and then pushed her away. "No!"

Once she had both kids strapped into the backseat of the car, she got in the driver's seat, sat there, and cried for 15 minutes. *Please God, have mercy.*

"Is this Captain Mercedes?"

"Who is calling?"

"Is this Captain Mercedes?"

"Yes, who are you?"

"I am Pablito Mendoza Garcia."

"Is this somebody's idea of a joke?"

"No. I really am Pablito Mendoza Garcia."

"How can you prove that?"

"Ms. Linda Neal, who you sent to us, was just here and I'm calling to check that she has safely returned."

"Yes, she has safely returned. Thank you for being kind to her."

"It was all my pleasure. I like her a lot."

"She also liked you a lot. From what she said, I would like to meet you."

"Why?"

"I'm not sure. I don't mean to sound condescending, but you are exotic. I want something different in my life and an exotic man on a mountaintop is certainly a change."

"That doesn't sound like a very good reason."

"It isn't. And I wouldn't do it for that reason. But I must admit, I did get more than a little bit envious of Linda as she described you."

"I don't know what she said, but I thought she was beautiful, intelligent, and charming."

"She thought you were handsome, intelligent, and charming. That's when I started getting a little envious."

"Is there any chance you can come down from the mountain so that I can meet you?"

"That doesn't seem realistic."

"I guess not. From her and from me, take care."

"Thank you."

The Chief, "What do we know about the massacre lady?"

"It appears to be sort of a hate crime. She belonged to a left-wing group, but they had kicked her out because she was too extreme for them. Apparently, she blamed religious Christians for slavery and other things she didn't like. She decided it was her responsibility to make them pay for their crimes."

Dave, "I've got to tell you chief; the massacre was at my church. I know every victim personally. I have prayed with every victim." You could hear the silent gasp in the room, followed by stunned silence.

The Chief stared at Dave. "Do you need to go home? Do you need help? We're here for you."

"Thank you, but I'm here to do my job." Again, there was a deafening silence.

"The killer is in custody. All the wounded are in the hospital. We've called in psychological support teams from all the hospitals, medical schools, and surrounding areas to help the families. I think we're doing everything that can be done."

"It scares the living shit out of me. Almost dozens of people dead for nothing. I'm supposed to give them a reason, or at least an explanation. What the hell do they pay me for? I don't understand it."

"I guess that's life, all of it. It's beyond understanding."

The chief slumped in his chair like an old man.

"OK, let's get back to the Alteman murder. Before we go off the deep end and start to take the craziness of some mystery force seriously, let's at least talk about this as a normal murder."

Mercedes, "I'm sorry sir, but the one thing it is not is a normal murder. It is a very complicated plot, and there is no plotter."

"What about the gambler?"

"Frank Agri gets a message he doesn't know from where. Now he says maybe it was a dream, maybe it was a phone call, but he doesn't remember. It's ridiculous. He takes about $35,000 in cash out of the receipts of one of his casinos and gives it in a box to Harry Gonzalez, who comes to pick it up. Why he gave it to a low-grade punk whom he doesn't know, he can't say. But he admits that he did it. We have retrieved some of the bills that Frank took from the casino. Some were still on Gonzalez when he died. The hooker who went to the guy operating the hotel night surveillance, and that guy, still had some. I'm sure a little bit ended up with the Salvadoran maid, who cleaned up the room, but we can't check on that. We can be reasonably certain that all the money came from Frank's casino."

"What does Gonzalez say?"

"We never got to talk to Gonzalez. He was in the hospital by the time the murder was committed, and he died later that night. It seems that night he went out, bought a lot of drugs, and got the shit beat out of him. All we know is what he told the people in the emergency room when the police brought him in. The docs say he was babbling relatively incoherently, and so they paid no real attention to what he said. But when we asked them to try to remember, there were a few points that came through. One is that he got the money. Two is that he bought a gun and stashed it near the hotel. And three, he put some of the money in an envelope under the door of a cheap apartment as he was told."

"This sounds like a bad story, not a real murder. Why do you believe any of it?"

"Because we can trace the bills and because the guy who turned off the surveillance cameras was so scared I was afraid he was going to shit all over the room. And the hooker was too dumb to lie."

"Next the cowgirl arranges to meet him that night at the hotel. And then she changes her mind. She gives no real reason why she made the date that particular night, and she gives no reason why she canceled, and no real reason why she didn't care that he never got the message she was canceling."

"Then the hooker goes and gets the surveillance guy to turn off the cameras."

"Who told her to do that?"

"She doesn't know. There was just a message under her door. She didn't keep the message, so we can't examine it. She brings the night surveillance guy to her apartment and gives him his half of the money and a good time."

"So then?"

"So then someone picks up the gun where it was stashed, probably along with the key to the room they got from the maid, goes to the room, gets in with no difficulty, commits the murder, cleans up the dead man, the gun and the room, drops the gun in the trash, and then goes God knows where."

"And who did the murder?"

"We don't know. The best bet now is that it was a woman from Chiapas called Angela, who seems to have flown here just to do the murder, and then return. She did it all with fake documents and in disguise. But the bigger question is not who pulled the trigger, but who and how the murder was organized. All of our suspects are suspects because we think they wanted Ted Alteman dead. They are candidates to be the person who organized the murder much more than the person who actually killed Ted Alteman. Whether or not they have alibis to be the murderer doesn't matter, if they are guilty of organizing the murder. None of them could plausibly organize this plot."

"Here's the list of liars with no alibi. Caroline Alteman, the widow, lied, both about her relationship with a dead man, she was, in fact, bitter about his neglecting her, and her relationship with Mr. Rathbone, the head of the law office. Rathbone lied about his efforts to romance the widow before the murder.

Tyrone Neal - plenty of motive, no alibi, and lied that he had gotten over his wife's infidelity.

Frank Agri lied that he didn't know anything about the murder, when, in fact, he paid for the gun. Alteman's other girlfriends are clear.

We tracked the cowgirl's cell phone, and the cell phone of the man she said she was with, and they were both at her ranch that night.

The doctor down in Monterey and her husband, the contractor, similarly were together that night. Gulov is dead, and there's no evidence that he or his partners were involved. Admittedly, they had a motive, and we have this wild call out of nowhere from Israel, claiming that an Israeli gangster said he would do the killing. But there's no evidence to connect them. Also, Linda Neal has no real alibi, but she has cooperated with us so much, that none of us believe she murdered him. And it's even more far-fetched to implicate her live-in boyfriend."

"So even if one of them instigated the murder, it seems that they didn't do it personally. They would have arranged for the murder gun to be delivered, so that the murderer, otherwise uninvolved in the case, could pick it up, do the job, and then dispose of it."

"And whoever arranged the murder, also arranged to have the surveillance cameras turned off. This is a very well-planned murder. It does not feel like a crime of passion."

"I think you put your finger right on the point. It is the plan which is the murder. It's not the finger that pull the trigger, not the money that bought the gun, nor getting the surveillance cameras turned off. It is whoever planned it all."

"All of our suspects, including the ones that lied and have no alibi, were not the planners. They were the pawns being manipulated by the planner."

"And there is no good candidate for that planner. And there's no obvious way that the planner got all the people to play their role. That's what's crazy. The plot is too big for any of the suspects."

"Don't tell anyone I said this, but I think we need to go public in search of this so-called 'queen'. But do it in such a way that they can't trace it back to us. We will look like idiots or worse."

"Linda Neal has already told us that's impossible. The queen is not a person or a thing, but a force beyond understanding."

Tyrone called Caroline and asked her to meet him for lunch. *Why? Why now? What does he want? I don't see how I can say no.*

"You know, in all the years I worked with Ted in the same office, I don't think I've met you more than two or three times, and that only for a few seconds at Christmas parties."

"It's true, but it's not just you. I have very little contact with the other people in the office."

"I did hear that you talk to Solly."

"Yes, I did. He's a friend."

"Well, that's not why I asked to meet you today. I assume you know, because everyone knows, that Ted had an affair with my ex-wife, and that led to our divorce."

"Yes, I do know. I even sort of knew it at the time."

"Did it affect your marriage?"

"Not really. The truth is your ex-wife was only one of many. There were others before her and after. Your ex was exceptional only in that I knew who she was. I never knew anything about most of the others."

"How did you know?"

"Well at the least, Solly told me when you had a fight in his office. But I was pretty sure before then. She called him at home several times. I didn't have to be a genius to figure it out. None of the others ever made any contact. I think they didn't know who he was. He often used fake identities."

"That's the part I need to understand. That's why I'm here. At the office, he was just a brilliant lawyer. Extremely smart, and even hard-working. He could be arrogant and nasty, but he behaved like a regular man. He didn't even try to hit up on the secretaries."

"In all the years I knew Ted the only thing he never was, was an ordinary or regular man. He was always at the extreme. He could be very sweet and he could be very cruel but I never saw him act like an ordinary man. He could be a devoted father and he could disappear for days forgetting his own children's birthdays or other events, and then treat his absence as if it was nothing."

"You think Linda was just another conquest. Just another opportunity to have a good time. He didn't care about her."

"I'm pretty sure he didn't care about her in the sense of having any real personal affection. I don't think he did for any of the women he went to bed with. In the end I don't think he had any real affection for me. But it's not true that she was just another. He cared a lot about getting her."

"How do you know?"

"Well again, the simplest is that she is the only one who knew who he was. He never let any of the other women know who it was so that they could have any leverage on him. He must've wanted her very badly to have put himself at risk in a way that he did with no one else."

"Why did he want her so much?"

"As you know, better than me, she is very beautiful. And of course, there's you. Ted was always very competitive. He thought you were brilliant, and therefore a competitor, and therefore he wanted to beat you."

"She is very beautiful. She had a lot of practice telling men to get lost. Why did he succeed when so many others had failed?"

"That's the mystery. That's the mystery. Ted was a completely different man before I met him, and during the time we were together he changed very dramatically. I never understood how or why."

Tyrone looked at her, his eyes begging for answers.

"When I met him, I fell for him like a ton of bricks. It was like nothing before in my life. And after we were married, I couldn't remember why I liked him. I admired him. And you could truly say I loved him. But I never understood where that feeling came from and how it seemed to disappear into nothing."

"Tell me more! That must've been what he did to Linda. What was it like?"

"I don't know. I just don't know. I've tried many times to remember and I can't. If you want to be vulgar, you could say I was in heat. You could say my hormones were out of control. You could say I was being childish, like a teenager. I don't know. I just don't know."

"And what happened then?"

"We were married. He made a lot of money. He was attentive to me and to our children. But he always said there was another side. That he would fool around if he wanted, and that he would come and go as he wanted, without any explanation."

"How do you accept that?"

"I did. Maybe I shouldn't have. I was in love. And in a sense, I had nothing to complain about. I was almost proud that a man who could have so many women so easily came home to me. But slowly things changed, little by little. He was less attentive, spent less time with us, and started showing more and more of his cruel side. Not towards us, but towards others in our presence. It served as a warning. If we did not behave, and accept things as he wanted them to be, then he could turn on us. We obeyed, and he never turned the cruelty on us."

"You know we're both suspects. We both had good reasons."

"I know. But I am innocent, and from the very little I know about you, I'm sure you're innocent also. I don't have much respect for the police, but I think they will realize that also."

"Let's hope so."

CHAPTER 34

SUSPECTS

"It's been a long time."

"Yes, indeed."

"Thank you for meeting me."

"Just because I turned you down, doesn't mean you're not an interesting man."

The mayor had suggested that they meet in this small café in Tomales Bay where no one would recognize them.

"On one hand, Mrs. Neal ..."

"It was Linda when you asked me for a date. You can use Linda now."

"Linda, we are all grateful for your help and impressed with your bravery in going to Chiapas. But on the other hand, you are a suspect. A very reasonable suspect to have committed murder, and you don't have an alibi."

"It doesn't sound like you're asking for a date this time. What do you want?"

"Well let's just start with the obvious. Did you do it? Do you know how it was done?"

"Let me tell you this. I was a kid in the backwoods of Kentucky with no future. Tyrone appeared like a half-man half-god. He had left our area and became rich, yet he came back to find a wife. He took me, a girl from nowhere, and gave me an education, a palace to live in, a glorious family, and a devoted sexy husband. I showed my appreciation by having an affair, disparaging him, and flaunting it. I hate myself, but I can't die, and I have to wake up each morning and look in the mirror at the bitch who humiliated a prince. If killing Ted would get me a smile from Tyrone, I would do it in an instant. But it wouldn't and I didn't. If you want to convict me, go ahead. You can't punish me more than I think I deserve. But if you want to find the actual killer, you'll have to look elsewhere."

"It appears that many people played a role in the murder, without knowing each other, without knowing the role they were playing, and without knowing who was orchestrating the murder. Do you understand that after your visit to Chiapas?"

"Mostly no, but a little bit of yes. It's very strange the way they work. Pablito is the boss, but he doesn't seem to give any orders. He doesn't know how they defeated the Mexican army. Rather it seems, the Mexican army defeated itself. I would guess that he and Angela were lovers. And I'm pretty sure that she would do anything he told her to do. But I don't think he told her to kill Ted. But I would bet money that she is the woman who came through Guatemala City, and then returned and there's no other reason for her to do it, except to commit the murder. And it's quite impossible that she had anything to do with the other features of the murder, such as getting him there."

"How does that work?"

"I don't know. All I do know is that while I was there I had wild and crazy dreams as if I was being examined and evaluated by forces beyond my imagination. They said I passed and that now, I would understand. But I don't understand, but maybe I will someday. I think they have all had that kind of dream and felt that they were inducted into some mysterious brotherhood. And I think they feel they get directions from the brotherhood. I know it sounds crazy but it's the best I can do."

"Linda, you are still an amazing ..."

"Thanks. I need all the flattery I can get. Did Ted put you up to it?"

"Yes, but it didn't take much. You are very pretty. He said you were available."

"It must've been just after the end of the affair."

"I'm sure it was. Ted's was not the kind of man to share a woman."

"You're attractive enough, but I needed time to heal."

"Lucky for me you turned me down. It would've destroyed my marriage. It was crazy to even ask."

"Mrs. Alteman, we know you lied. We know that you've been seeing Mr. Rathbone for at least a year."

"I'm sorry. I shouldn't have done it. I know."

"Then why did you?"

"For the obvious reason, I was embarrassed. I'm actually a very proper woman."

"You realize it's very suspicious. It makes you a prime suspect. A prime suspect of having committed murder."

"I didn't do it. And although I was lonely, and hurt, I would not have wanted to do it. When I said that other women threw themselves at him, it's the truth. And when I said, I was proud that he always came home to me, it's the truth. I admit I enjoyed the fact that Solly loved me. I enjoy it now. I used to think when this was all over, maybe I would be with Solly. But I didn't want to see Ted dead."

"We think the murder involved several people who did not know each other. Who were organized to commit murder by someone else. Who do you think that could be?"

"I don't know. As I said, Ted led a very mysterious life. I wasn't a part of that mysterious life, but I could see it lots of times."

"What does that mean?"

"The most obvious is that all the women he was having didn't know who he was. Not one of them out of jealousy or anything else tried to contact me. If they knew who he was, at least one of them would have tried. But that's not all. Sometimes, when we went to a party, people would talk to him about very big things, but they would always do it in a way that never revealed what they were talking about. He and the other person knew, but they had some coded, mysterious understanding that they did not want me, or anybody else to share."

"Did you ever see him use a false identity?"

"Yes. Two or three times when we went on a trip to South America or Africa, we used fake passports for both of us. They showed us as husband and wife, but not a real identity. We used our American passports when we left and returned home."

"Why weren't you suspicious?"

"One can always be suspicious. In every aspect of life, there are the things you can see, and the things you can't see. When some things happen in the government or in other countries and they don't make sense to you, people believe that there are hidden forces at work. Sometimes people laugh at that belief and call it a conspiracy theory. Sometimes it turns out to be true. I don't want to offend you, but it is a fact that our government lies, even frequently. They tell us it's for our good, and maybe it is. But I don't know. Do you? And then there were coincidences. I have a friend who went to a party that she was not expected to go to and met the love of her life. The man was not supposed to go to the party either. What do you call that?"

"But this is a murder, not falling in love."

"I'm sorry I lied. I hope you believe me. But I do know that some conspiracy theories turn out to be true."

"I have to admit that this meeting is probably illegal and certainly inappropriate. If you want to leave you can. The guards will take you back to your cell. I am the mayor. I'm here with the chief of police and Officer Dave Good. Let me tell you again, you can leave at any time. We are here because the people you massacred all belong to Officer Good's church. We want to understand why you did it."

"Go to hell!"

"You don't want to talk to us?"

"I don't mind talking to you, just so you know that I despise self-righteous shit like you."

"You don't know any of the people you murdered. Why didn't you just put a little more effort into finding out who you wanted to kill?"

"I did. I picked out a church filled with self-righteous white people. You live off slavery and you think you're virtuous. That's what I call scum."

"Let's go, Dave. She's crazy. There's no satisfaction to be gained from talking to a crazy person."

"I am commanded by my Lord Jesus Christ to forgive you. But I can't. The people you killed were all good people. Not one of them lived off slavery. All of them worked hard and were loving to everyone around them. You deserve to die, but instead, they will put you in a mental hospital and take care of you for the rest of your life. It's not right."

The mayor looked at Dave and said to the guards, "Take her back to her cell." After the prisoner left, "I feel dirty having just been in the same room with that thing."

CHAPTER 35

STRAWS IN THE WIND

"I'm quitting my job."

Krishna led Mercedes into his study. Although the pictures and the other decorative articles in the room were from India, the room itself was from central Europe. Dark wood panels, heavy drapes, and a deep warm chair that you could just sink into. It was as close to the womb as any adult could ever get.

"Are you serious?"

"Totally serious. I've decided it's time to make some big changes in my life. It has nothing to do with my job, my family, or anything like that. I must admit this last case has been difficult. I can't tell what it is or why, but I'm not comfortable. But that's not the reason. I need to make a change."

"Family? Men?"

"Family, no. I think I'm going to move and I feel bad about leaving them. They're elderly and I owe them so much. But maybe men. I've had a few recently that just didn't work out. I'm not getting younger. The real reason is that my life lacks meaning and focus. I just am moving forward without knowing where or why."

Krishna smiled. *I could not love her more if she was my daughter by blood. But for sure, she is my daughter in her soul.* "You cannot know where or why. That is not given to human beings. But to want to know where and why is the glory of a well-led life. I am so proud of you."

Mercedes basked in the warmth of his love. Her soul melted and was purely open. "I need your advice. I trust you more than anyone. Tell me how to proceed."

"I can't do that. Whatever words I use would have different meanings to me than to you. I derive my meaning, starting from my life in India as a man. You derive your meaning, starting as an infant in a Mexican family in America. But, even if we had very similar backgrounds, no two people can know that the same word about the deep issues of life has the same meaning for them, and for someone else. The same words would have different meanings."

"Then what do I do?"

"You try. That's all any of us can do. And if you feel that a change is the way to try, then make the change. But do it with an open heart and an open mind so that you can find the road that you feel gives your life focus and meaning."

"Linda, after all, you've been through, after all we've been through together, I think of you as a friend and I like you very much. But I'm not here as your friend. I'm here as a cop. I'm here to investigate you for the murder of Ted. For a lot of reasons, we think the murder was done by several people working together. You don't have much of an alibi, but that's not what we are focused on. We are focused on the group that organized the murder."

"Ask me anything."

"I can't protect you, but I would like to believe you'll tell me the truth. Did you have anything to do with the murder? Do you know anything about the murder except what you learned in Chiapas?"

"Nothing. I swear to you, I know nothing."

"I choose to believe you. "

"Thank you."

"How well did you know Caroline Alteman?"

"Not very well at all. We met a few times at Christmas parties and other business social events but that's all. To be blunt, she's not my kind of lady."

"What does that mean?"

"She's too much the good girl. I'm not a bad girl but I don't like good girls. I think she's a fake. I don't know anything bad about her, but she's too well-behaved for my taste. The other thing is, they were all very successful lawyers and made a lot of money, but Ted made more and Caroline flaunted it. I wouldn't have wanted to flaunt it, even if Tyrone were making as much as Ted."

"What about his other women?"

"I've told you everything I know."

"What about Harris? He was supposed to see her the night she was killed."

"I don't know anything about her. After Ted dumped me, I was more than a little jealous of her. I did find out that she had more than a few men herself. I took solace in the idea that she would do to Ted what he did to me."

"I will begin today's sermon with death. I will end today's sermon with life. This is what our Lord Jesus Christ has taught us.

We are here today to mourn the death of 33 of our brothers and sisters. They are all literally the brothers and sisters of many of you here today who survived the massacre. They are also the brothers and sisters of all of you in faith, who have been here and prayed with them so many Sundays. And they were also the brothers and sisters of millions of people outside these walls, who have never met them, for we are all God's children. From the moment we were born, we knew that we would all die. That is why we begin with death.

Do not shy away from the pain in your heart. Do not try to forget it. Rather wrap your arms around it. It is that pain that makes you human. It is that pain that joins you to all of us. It is that pain that gives you the path to salvation. It is the pain that gives you the path to the meaning of life. It is that pain, which is the enduring soul of the departed. It is that pain that touches God's love for you. Wrap your arms around that pain. Not to become depressed and give up on the joys, the hopes, the disappointments, and all the rest of life, but rather to bring yourself closer to the transcendent meaning of life in faith.

The power of God is not in your body but in your soul. Our brothers and sisters have been deprived of their body, but we of faith know that they have not been deprived of their soul. But even those who lack faith can see that these fallen live on in our hearts. The mask of the human form has been stripped away by the murderer, we can see the real life clearly. Close your eyes, praise God, and see the enduring lives of our brothers and sisters. May we all thus live forever.

CHAPTER 36

STRANGE CONNECTIONS

Tyrone made an appointment to see Mercedes in her office.

"I have some information for you and I want some information from you."

"You can tell me what you have, but I won't promise to give you anything that I have. Police information is not available on request."

"I'm not worried. What I have for you is quite simple. I have proof that I could not have committed the murder. I remembered that I withdrew money from an ATM in Sonora at 9:02PM the night of the murder, while I was on the trip that I intended for fishing. Here is the receipt that I download from the Internet. And I'm sure that the ATM took my picture while I was standing there. So you have a positive identification."

Mercedes looked at the receipt. "It looks pretty good to me. We'll send it to the bank for the picture identification. And what did you want from me?"

"I believe you and Linda are now friends."

"I would like to think so. As I told you, I admire what she did, going to Mexico."

"And what should she have done in Mexico?"

"What do you mean? You know she went to see El Sueño, the drug lord."

"And what did she do while she was there?"

"I don't know. I wasn't there and I didn't ask."

"What did you surmise from your conversations?"

"What are you getting at?"

"What was her relationship to the drug lord?"

"I think you're jealous."

"I hate her. She destroyed my life. She trampled all over me. I hate her."

"I think you do, but I also think you still love her. I think you're jealous."

"What was her relationship to the drug lord?"

"I do know that they spent a lot of time together. That's what she was sent to do. I know that she learned to call him by his real name, Pablito, not the name the police use."

"What did she say about him?"

"She said he was not especially handsome, but he was a very interesting man. Not at all what she expected of a drug lord."

"What else?"

"What do you want?"

"I want to know if they had an affair"

"I don't know."

"What do you think?"

"I think they did."

"And why do you think that?"

"Just the sound of her voice. To be honest, she sounded in love. In fact, she made him sound so interesting, I was a little envious of her."

"That's not what I wanted to hear."

"You asked for my opinion, and I gave it. I might be wrong."

"I don't think so. She's the kind who does what she wants regardless of the consequences."

"I've been assured that everything I tell you is confidential."

"We will do everything we can, Dr. Mason, to keep the information you give us confidential. But there are no legal guarantees."

"Do you understand my problem?"

"We understand that you will tell us that you spent the night with Ms. Sally Harris at her ranch and that you don't want your wife to know."

"Exactly."

"We do want it under oath"

"I'll do what I have to. But please, don't destroy my life."

"It's not just that you spent the night with her, but when and why she made the arrangements that you did."

"What do you want to know?"

"When did you make the arrangements for that night?"

"As best as I can remember, sometime in the afternoon my wife called me in my office to say that she had been invited by one of her friends to come to some big party they were having in Las Vegas for a movie star who was a friend of my wife's friend. The invitation came with no warning. And I think it was close to 4 o'clock before she called me to tell me that she was on her way to the airport. I realized it was an opportunity I didn't want to miss to be with Sally. I hadn't been able to find an opportunity for weeks. I've known Sally for years and we've had this relationship for years. I see her when I can. She understands that. So when I called her, she said she'd have to break some plans she made that day and that she would. And she did."

"Do you have any proof?"

"I can get you a copy of my wife's ticket to Las Vegas and you can see that it was not booked until that afternoon."

"That should work."

The chief walked into the interrogation room. *I need to break this guy.* "You were brought here because we are going to put you under arrest, Frank. Your fingerprints are all over the murder of Ted Alteman. We think you arranged it, and I think we can get a conviction."

"Never mind that, I didn't do it."

"You didn't pull the trigger, but you paid for the gun and the killer. That's murder."

"I have no idea what you're talking about. I've told you all I know about Ted Alteman."

"Why did you take the $35,000 out of your casino account?"

"I don't know. It came over me the way other things have come over me, and I did it. It wasn't the first time I did something like that, that I didn't understand. And I'm sure it won't be the last. As I told you before, I felt it came from the queen."

Slimy bastard. "I'm tired of this queen crap. That's just bullshit that you're trying to sell me with your friend in Mexico. I don't believe a word of it."

"It's not bullshit. On the grave of my mother, it's the truth. I swear to God."

"Prove it."

"I can't, it's impossible."

"Then I don't believe you, and you're under arrest."

Frank just stared at him. "I don't know what I can do, but I'll try. You don't really have a case against me, so give me a week."

"OK, but if you try to get away with something, I swear, I'll fry your ass."

"Mrs. Neal said you would talk to me."

"Since her visit, Linda is a friend of mine. She asked me to talk to you, and I said I would. I admit, I don't usually speak to police chiefs."

"She said to call you Pablito."

"That is what I prefer."

"Pablito, as you know, we are investigating the murder of Ted Alteman. Can you help us?"

"I don't know. Ask me a question, and I'll do my best."

"Do you know who killed him?"

"No, I don't know."

"Can you make a good guess?"

"I can make a poor guess. I take a good guess to mean I know, but I don't have proof. That's not the case. A poor guess is, I don't know, but I do know some related things, which affect the probabilities."

God, he does sound like a philosopher. "We are more than a little bit desperate. I would appreciate your poor guess."

"As you know, the Mexican government sent a part of the army to attack us on this hill, but they failed. As you know equally well, we did not have, and do not have the resources to stand up to the Mexican army. Somehow, the army became so confused and disorganized that they started to fire on each other until they were so successful at destroying themselves that they withdrew. I have experience with events like that in my life that are supremely important to me and are at first consideration incomprehensible. What do you do when you have similar events that are both important and incomprehensible?"

"I don't know what to say. I don't know what you want me to say."

"Before the army attacked, I had decided to surrender. Our situation was impossible, and I did not want to be responsible for the needless death. But then, as I was falling asleep, I had the most powerful feeling, you could call it a dream, or maybe it was just my wish, or something else, but I felt that I should not surrender, and that somehow things would work out. We prepared to fight and did, but we were nothing compared to the army. Things did work out. It's not the only time in my life when I have had that kind of hunch, dream, or whatever you want to call it. And usually, it has worked out. My friends tell me that it is the will of God. But I don't believe in God. Some people tell me I'm lucky, but what does that mean?"

"Do those hunches come from what they call the queen?"

"I don't know what people mean by the queen, except if there are people like me, who have had things work out for which there is no other explanation. From what I've been told Ted was one of those people. Until he wasn't, and his luck run out."

"Someone bought the gun that killed him. Someone pulled the trigger that killed him. Someone arranged the room after he was dead, including changing his clothes. That's not luck, that's a conspiracy."

"Like I said, things happen that make no sense, except that they do. Take it or leave it."

"Did Angela kill him?"

"I don't know, but probably. I know she went away for a day, and I now know that that was the day that Ted was killed. I think Angela is a good guess."

"We will want to arrest her."

"You can try, but I doubt that you'll be more successful than the Mexican army."

CHAPTER 37

WHAT DO WE KNOW?

The mayor was not happy. He convened a meeting of everyone who might be able to help him with the Alteman case. "I'm getting the shit beat out of me about this case. I need to get ahead of the curve. What do we know and what do we not know?"

The chief, "Let's start from the end and work backwards. We know that we're dealing with a dead man named Theodore Alteman. He has been positively identified both by sight of him by people who knew him and by fingerprints and other markers. We know that he was killed with a gun. It had been wiped clean and thrown into a large trash bin. We were lucky that we sealed off the site almost immediately, and the bin was not emptied. We have recovered the gun and ballistics match. We know that he was shot with four bullets, and believe that the bullet to the head and to the groin were gratuitous after he was dead, although we can't be exactly sure of the sequence of bullets."

The mayor was extremely intent. "And we believe from the choice of gun, and the bullet to the groin, that the murderer was a woman. Correct?"

"Correct. We also know that the murder was meticulously planned to make it impossible for us to find the killer. And whoever planned it, has so far succeeded in that. If it wasn't obvious from everything else, the fact that he was found fully dressed, in clothes

215

that he did not wear there and which showed no signs of the murder, makes it painfully evident."

Mercedes added, "I think that understates the point. He wasn't just fully dressed, and they weren't just not the clothes he wore when he came in, and it wasn't just that there was no sign of the murder visible when he was found, but we believe that the cleanup was done after the killer had left. Whoever organized the murder, arranged for the cleanup also. It is the organizer of the murder, who is the real murderer."

The mayor, "Who did the clean-up?"

"Almost for certain it was one of the housekeeping staff who has since fled the country."

"He didn't go there to get killed. How did they do it?"

The chief, "There are three separate parts to that. And it's more than possible that each part is associated with a different person. The first part is why did he go there? The second is who gained access to the room to kill him and then did kill him? And the third is, who cleaned up the mess and left him looking so perfect? I think that all three were different women."

"Why all women?"

Dave, "He had a weakness for women."

The chief, "They are neat and careful. But of course, we don't know."

"No clues?"

"We think we know why he went there, but there's a problem with it. One of his girlfriends called him up and suggested they meet at the hotel. But then she backed out and didn't go. She has an ironclad alibi. She was with a different man."

"Then why did she set him up?"

"She says she had no intention of setting him up. She just planned a romantic evening and then changed her mind. They say women have a right to change their mind."

"That's weird and very suspicious."

Mercedes, "As you'll see, those kinds of weird and superficially coincidental events are all over this case."

"As for the last one, one of the maids at the hotel, who would have had a key to the room, is originally from El Salvador, may have been illegal, and has disappeared. We questioned people who knew her and they think she got a lot of money just before the killing. She went by the name, Silvana Gomez, but there is reason to believe that's not her real name. We have sent communications to the government in El Salvador. They located a woman who had returned from the United States with an unexpected amount of money. They sent us a picture of her, and although no one is quite sure, some witnesses believe it is the woman who was the hotel maid. At our request, they have interrogated her, but so far they have found nothing."

"Who told her what to do? Where did she get the money?"

"She has committed no obvious crime, so there is a limit to what the Salvadorans will do. We're pretty sure the money came from Frank Agri. And we are guessing that the instructions came from the person who organized the murder."

"And why did Agri agree to give her the money?"

"We don't know. He said it just came to him as a feeling, but he doesn't remember. He also gave the money to buy the gun."

"It sounds like Agri is the killer. He's the one that organized the murder."

"I wish it were, but as I'll explain, it's not possible."

"OK, what about Agri and the gun?"

"Agri gave money to a local petty crook named Harry Gonzalez. We're pretty sure that Gonzales left the gun behind the trash. Harry must've gotten a lot of money because he went out and bought a lot of drugs and died the same night of an overdose. As I said, we can't be sure of a lot of this because the surveillance system was turned off."

"Son of a bitch. How is that possible?"

"What we do know is that a hooker who worked that hotel frequently went to see the guy who monitored the surveillance cameras, and offered him money, and a free one with her if he would turn off the cameras. He took the offer. She told us that she got the money and the instructions slipped under the door of her apartment. She has no idea how they got there. It seems likely it was put there by Harry Gonzalez."

"So Agri organized the killing, and Gonzalez carried it out, including pulling the trigger."

"No. Gonzalez was dead from drugs before the murder."

"We don't know for sure who got the hooker to get the surveillance system turned off, or who had paid the maid who cleaned up the room, but it's more than likely Harry Gonzalez. If it wasn't him, it was probably someone just like him."

"Then who did the killing, and who organized the killing?"

"This is where it starts to get mysterious. Agri has a relationship with someone very powerful and is commonly known as the queen. We have no idea who that is, but we think it is connected to El Sueño. One of the dead man's former girlfriends managed to get herself to meet El Sueño. He more or less told her that he sent an agent to do the murder, and he made some of the arrangements."

"Have you spoken to El Sueño?"

"Are you kidding me? The Mexican army could not get to talk to him. Why he agreed to talk to this lady is not clear."

"What else did she learn?"

"As best as she could tell, one of the women who live with El Sueño on the mountaintop probably just drove to Guatemala City, took an airplane to San Francisco, took a cab to the hotel, picked up the gun where it had been placed, went to the room, knocked on the door, when he opened it, shot him, and then, after dropping the gun in the trash, retraced her steps back to the mountaintop."

"And who is that woman?"

"She's known in the compound as Angela. That's all we know."

"At root, El Sueño ordered the murder."

"Why?"

"That is the mystery at the heart of the mystery. All we know is what the dead man's girlfriend tells us. And frankly, it's not clear if she knows anything. My sense is that she fell in love with him down there. All she tells us is that there is a force, sometimes called the queen, that can make people do things by putting ideas in their head."

"El Sueño works for the force, the queen, or whatever you call it?"

"Not exactly. Again, the lady is not very clear, but as best as I can tell, it is a fluid relationship. El Sueño is under their influence. When they put ideas in his head, he recognizes them as having come from the queen, the force, and unless there's a good reason otherwise, he does what they want. In exchange, they protect him. It seems like when the Mexican army tried to capture him, the force drove the Mexicans so crazy that they ended up shooting at each other until they ran out of soldiers and ammunition. The government was so embarrassed that they gave up and they just left him in peace on his mountaintop."

"You know chief, if I hadn't known you all these years, I would say you were crazy."

"Mayor, if my family didn't reassure me when I get home, I would say I was crazy."

"Shit!"

"In summary, the woman who set him up has an ironclad alibi. The man who delivered the murder weapon is dead. The murderess is unreachable on a Mexican mountaintop. The woman who cleaned up has disappeared into El Salvador. The hooker who got the surveillance system turned off is worthless. And that's the easy part. The hard part is that there's a mastermind of the whole plot."

Everyone was silent.

"You know, I've had been thinking about the Alteman case in the context of that mass murder. In both of them, we are supposed to accept that there are things that we don't know. Worse than that, we are supposed to accept that we can't know. I don't like it, but I guess I could learn to live with it. But the Alteman case has one big difference. It is not just one event we can't understand, but the coordination of multiple events that we can't understand. It means you can't look at it as some random event. It has to be driven by some intelligence. I don't know how to deal with that."

"You're not the only one. No one does."

"OK, so who are the good candidates to be the mastermind?"

"There are on only two real candidates for the mastermind, Gulov, and the queen."

"The obvious one is Frank. It's his money that drove the whole operation."

"And maybe he's just the intermediate for the really big boys like Gulov and people associated with him. Yes, they had 1 billion good reasons to kill him, and murder comes naturally to them. Also, we still have that crazy call about an Israeli."

"What about a combo of the two lawyers Rathbone and Neal? They both hated him, and they are more than smart enough to put together a plot."

"Why not revenge of the women? All of them; his wife, Sally Harris who set him up, a vengeful dumped Linda Neal, and maybe even the Salvadoran maid he might've hit up on."

"They are all wild ideas, but the last one is too much!"

"Why? They could genuinely feel he had it coming. Even I think he had it coming."

"OK, we have three theories: the big boys, the colleagues, and the women. Certainly, we need to check the big boys. At the least, Frank has admitted to being an accessory to murder. We should be able to get more out of him. And while we're at it, check out the Israeli."

"We can call each of the lawyers separately and simply accuse them. See what they say."

"That sounds reasonable to me."

"I don't see how to check out the women, especially the widow. If she's not guilty, we look pretty ugly."

Mercedes, "I'll do the former Mrs. Neal and the widow."

"We got to do it, but I'm telling you right now, it's going to fail. There are too many working parts to this plot for any of those possibilities to put it together. It's dead in the water before it starts. I'll say it again, there are only two real candidates for the mastermind, Gulov, and the queen."

"I hate to say this, but I think you're right. But if we don't find one of them, then we're left with the crazy stuff."

"It is crazy stuff."

They all just looked at each other, unwilling to face the consequences of that conclusion.

CHAPTER 38

CLOUDS

Frank Agri insisted that only the mayor and the chief be present and that they come to his house. Reluctantly, they agreed. "I won't deny I was scared. I'm not afraid of you, and I'm not even afraid of prison, but I am afraid of what some of my so-called friends would do if I were out of action for a while. I don't believe in God, and I didn't pray, but I did ask for help, and it came. I have some people I want you to meet. After that, you can do what you want." Frank walked to the other side of the room and opened the door. In walked Marianne Grande; the mayor and the chief recognized her immediately.

"Ms. Grande!?"

"Do you like my music?" Both men in unison affirmed. "Mr. Agri called my manager and asked me to come and tell you about a few things that happened in my life and changed everything. I don't know Mr. Agri, and I don't know why he wants me to tell you this. But I just got a feeling I should do it and so I came." It was hard to tell if they were paying rapt attention to what she said, or simply ogling the gorgeous, famous singer. "I got married when I was 17. It wasn't long before he was raping me every night and then beating me black and blue. All I knew was to be terrified and cry. And then a better man, I don't know today if it really happened, or it was just a dream, but he told me he loved me and he cared for me. He told me to be brave. He told me to leave my husband and he would look after me. I asked him for his name, but all he would say was, I should call him my prince. I did what he said, and within a month I had a job in a recording studio as a secretary, and about a year later I was a star."

"Are you saying that her prince is like your queen?"

"I think so."

"About six months or a year after I had left my husband, he was found dead. The police said they thought it was a drug deal gone bad, but they didn't know and no one was ever charged. I believe in my heart, that my prince took care of it to protect me."

"Ms. Grande, you said there was more?"

"I probably shouldn't tell you this. A few years later, while I was on tour, I met a guy and I guess you could say he did a good job of romancing me for a couple of days. Then he asked me to do him a favor. My next stop was Houston and he asked me to deliver a package to his friend. I did. A couple of months later I read that his friend was arrested as a major cocaine distributor. I have no doubt I was a mule. I never saw him again, and to this day, I don't know why I was so taken with him. I don't even remember liking him. It feels like magic, alien."

"What does that have to do with the queen?"

"When something like what happened with my prince happens to you, I think you get used to following feelings that you don't know where they come from, but you just do it."

Both men started to squirm as they realized where this was going.

"And then there was my automobile accident. I was driving home from visiting my mother on a small country road when a car came the other way, at full speed on my side of the road. I remember the terror I felt up to the moment of impact. They tell me that one of us must've swerved at the last moment, so that instead of a head-on collision, I was sideswiped, and the car rolled over. I had broken arms, broken legs, and broken ribs but blessedly no brain damage.

I woke up in the hospital almost 8 hours later. But the thing I will never forget was while I was unconscious, I was visited by my prince, who made love to me, and told me that everything would be OK. And it was." Her voice broke, and she started to cry. In a few moments, she regained her composure, looked at the men, and walked out through the door through which she came without saying another word.

Frank, the mayor, and the chief looked at each other for a few moments, all a bit stunned. Then Frank started to walk towards a different door. "I have more." He opened the door, and as a well-dressed older man walked in, Frank said, "I don't know if either of you have ever met Congressman Hafner from Nebraska before."

"Gentleman." They all shook hands. "I've known Frank a long time, and he came and asked me to come and talk to you about the queen. I understand that if you've never met the queen, it's hard to understand. People who know the queen, don't talk about it probably because they think everyone else will think they're crazy. I'm not crazy, but the queen is as real as the nose on my face."

"You've had sex with her?"

Laughing, "No. She's real, but not like an ordinary person."

"Then, what is she?"

"She's someone you meet in your head. When I was a kid in college, I was a little bit smart and more than a little bit wild. I decided it would be cool to try psychedelic drugs. It was a lot of fun. It's just as well that most of my constituents don't know it, but a couple of times I guess I took too much, and I woke up in a hospital in restraints. One time, the police found me almost naked in the park, raving at the moon. That was when I met the queen. Some people will tell you it was just a drug-induced hallucination. And some people will tell you that the times I met her since then, are just flashbacks of my craziness. I don't see her anymore, and so maybe that's the right answer. But I will tell you, there is no part of my body, no furniture in my home, not one of the people I love in my family, who is any more real in my mind than she was, and still is."

"How do you know that your vision of the queen is the same as what Frank means when he tells us that she told him to do something?"

"I can't be sure, but still, I'm confident. Something is overwhelming when you meet the queen. You always remember that feeling and when you meet someone else who has had the same feeling, you can see it in their eyes. I have some very religious friends, and they feel the same way about other people who share their faith."

The remainder of the conversation was just friendly chatter, and then he left. They told Frank that they got the point, and that was enough. Frank insisted they had to hear one more testimony. "I did not contact this person. Somehow, they found out what was happening and called to me." The mayor and the chief looked at each other and nodded their heads.

A tall black man walked in, immaculately dressed. With a mild African accent, he said, "I am Ambassador Agremu." He handed them a copy of his diplomatic credentials. They shook hands, and then all sat down. "My president learned of this issue and wanted me to come and give you his testimony. I have been in the diplomatic service for 40 years and no one has ever asked me to do anything even remotely like this."

The Ambassador stopped for a moment and looked at the other men. "The president told me that for no obvious reason, he was reading press reviews from the United States, and came across this story. For some reason, he realized that at the center of the mystery, was what he called The Deep Spirit. He realized that you may call the Spirit by other names, or may not know The Spirit. He asked me to look into it, and I found out that Mr. Agri had arranged this meeting. The president told me to offer to come and he gave me very explicit instructions as to what to say."

"He must've seen one of the stories that we had placed in the papers."

"I don't know. What he wanted me to say, goes back to the time when I was born. My country was run by men who were worse than gangsters because since they controlled the government, they had no inhibition. A small group of very brave men went into the bush to build an army to overthrow the gangsters. My president was a teenager who joined them. The leader of that group is the most admired man in the history of my country. He taught his men that they were invincible, because The Deep Spirit supported them, and she would make sure they won."

"She?" the mayor and the chief said in unison.

"They always refer to The Deep Spirit in the feminine. ... But as the rebels got close to victory, that leader became more selfish and cruel. As it is told to me, the men were afraid to be without him, and they were afraid to be with him. My president is a brave and good man. He says that he wanted to kill the leader, but he was afraid. One day that leader went on a raid with a small group of men. When the men came back, they said they had gotten separated from the leader, and didn't know what had happened to him. He was found the next day dead, his body mutilated including his manhood. My president says that in the years since then, he has felt The Deep Spirit many times, and he is sure that she had him killed as he had become unjust."

"It may seem cruel, Mrs. Alteman, but you are a serious suspect. We don't believe you pulled the trigger. The murder of your late husband was a very complicated plot. Somebody organized the plot. You have plenty of motive, you do have money, and more than enough intelligence to organize a plot."

"I had nothing to do with it. I swear. I had nothing to do with it."

"We know you've been lying. We know about your relationship with Mr. Rathbone."

"I'm sorry. I regret lying. Solly, Mr. Rathbone, was very good to me when I got depressed over the way Ted was treating us. He also did an unbelievable job in recovering some of the money that Ted had hidden away just before he was killed. I believe Ted was going to leave me. Maybe I felt that way even before he was killed, so I leaned very hard on Solly and he supported me. I will always be grateful."

Caroline's mind flashed back to what happened when she went to her daughter's school performance. *I felt like a teenager.* It was a pure accident that she sat next to him in the audience. *I had worried about what to wear since everyone at the school knew that Ted had just died. But I thought, I hadn't died, and so I wore the bright pink dress and a few of my jewels. Then he called me to meet him for coffee the next day.*

"But you should know I broke up with him just a few days ago. I am young still, and I need a future. Solly is much too old to be my future. I had nothing to do with murder, and neither did Solly."

"What do you know about Sally Harris?"

"Who? Sally Harris? I never heard of her."

CHAPTER 39

FOR LOVE OF GOD

It was yet another one of those meetings in the mayor's office. No one was happy. The chief broke the silence. "We've hit the wall. None of the reasonable suspects by having a motive are reasonable suspects for organizing the murder plot ... with the possible exception of Gulov and his narco friends, since we can't investigate them. The only thing we are left with is the Frank Agri, El Sueño craziness of the queen."

The mayor, "I can't go there. It is crazy. They will laugh me out of town."

"We understand," Mercedes spoke up. "I think it's crazy also, but I have a friend, a very distinguished professor, who I believe can help us."

"There are a lot of crazy professors."

"I've known him all my life. He is a wonderful man and not at all crazy."

"Captain Mercedes has brought her professor friend here to explain it."

"He's not crazy, is he?"

"I don't think so. But I'll bring him in and let you decide for yourself."

Krishna walked in, and the mayor greeted him warmly. "The Chief and Captain Mercedes tell me that you can make sense of all this craziness."

"You've been misled. I can't do that. I believe I know some things that have been useful to me, and to millions of others and are too often neglected when we need them. Maybe I can help you to bring some good out of your problem."

"I appreciate your modesty. Please …". The mayor pointed to a large comfortable chair in a corner of the office.

"What I want to say to you is, I believe, both trivial and profound. It is just another way of looking at the obvious. But from what Mercedes has told me about your case, I believe it will make you comfortable in your predicament."

"You are going to get me to believe in magic?"

"You could say that. I would put it differently."

"I mean no disrespect professor, but I think you wasting your time and mine."

"I will leave if you prefer."

The chief, "Give him a chance. Even an old son-of-a-bitch like you can learn something."

"OK."

"As I understand it, the story of the murder that you have now is a mixture of facts you know, gaps of facts you cannot know, and claims you find ridiculous or unbelievable."

"Our job is to fill the gaps and get rid of the ridiculous."

"Have you ever had a case you didn't solve?"

"Of course."

"Did you ever have a case where you solved the murder but cannot imagine any good reason for the murder?"

"Of course."

"Have you ever had a case where you got a conviction, and later felt got the wrong person?"

"It's a little painful, but yes."

"Despite your best efforts, and let me be clear, I admire the work you do, you are very familiar with the fact that there's a lot of times you don't know the whole truth even when the case is over."

"What's your point?"

"I want to focus on the ideas and beliefs you use regarding things you don't know and you don't understand. We've just shown that there were many such things. Despite your best efforts, you don't know or even could be wrong. Nonetheless, you are comfortable, as you should be. The truth beyond our knowledge is everywhere in our environment."

"I still don't get your point. When I confront things I don't understand, I don't resort to magic."

"Oh, but you do. You do not call it magic. There are many things that you experience on a daily basis, based on modern technology, which every intelligent person for most of history would have called magic. At any one time, our civilization lives under the canopy of the extent of its knowledge. Things that lie outside of that canopy get called magic, accident, the work of God, and a variety of other words. Moses saw a burning bush that didn't burn up, Think of how simple that would've been for us to produce."

"Those technologies are based on facts. My confidence in them is based on facts. You're just peddling smoke and mirrors."

"You believe the murderer is protected by a wall the Mexican Army could not breach."

"Yes."

"How that is possible is a gap in your knowledge, a fact you cannot fill. Isn't that true?"

"Yes, of course. There are many things in the course of police work where you can't get all the facts you want. But there's nothing mysterious about that. It's just the way it is."

"So, you are fully adjusted to the existence of facts you do not understand, and will never understand."

"Exactly. So what does that have to do with mysterious magical powers?"

"I agree completely, but I just want to accommodate you to those portions of the truth that you do not have. These are portions of the truth, that you think you could have under different circumstances, but under the current circumstances, you can't get. Let me suggest to you that the entity they call the queen has advanced technology that allows them to influence the minds of human beings. And they can do it from some distant place, perhaps a planet on a distant solar system."

"That's just science fiction fantasy."

"What if I tell you that there are people who kill themselves, or have themselves killed, in order to join their loved ones in the next world?"

"I accept that some people are religious fanatics. But that's not a fact."

"It is a fact to them, and they think you're the fool not to know it."

"I can't go there."

"If you can't go to advanced technology, can you go to pure luck, coincidence?"

"Sure, I can go to coincidences, but this one is such an incredible collection of coincidences that it can't be just luck or bad luck for Alteman."

"How improbable does something have to be for it to be incredible do you? The great mathematician John Littlewood asked this question in a very careful mathematical and scientific way. He concluded that you could expect some kind of 'miracle' every 35 days. Maybe you can't go all the way to 35 days but can you go to 35 weeks or 35 months or 35 years? If you say, the things are just random events, then if you wait long enough, anything can happen. So are you a Littlewood man, a believer in random miracles?"

"This is not some collection of random events. A whole bunch of people were coordinated to make this happen. There is a mind that thought this through and got everyone to cooperate in a murder. That's not a collection of random events. Someone caused this to happen."

"Like most people, you believe in causality. When something happens, there's a cause. But that's a very tricky business. The more people think about it, the less clear it is. Some philosophers say that causality is an illusion. It's an illusion we like, but it's our invention, not a part of the world."

"That's crazy. If you believe that, then nothing in the world makes sense."

"You got it exactly. If you want to believe that things make sense, then you must believe in God."

"I don't believe in God. I was raised to believe in God, who told me when and where, why and how, and with whom I could have sex or something else. That's just superstition."

"I'm not telling you to change your mind, but you shouldn't be quite so quick. A lot of very smart people believe in God. Most of them don't think he's an old man sitting up in heaven, judging you for how you act with women. It's a lot more sophisticated than that, but it is God"

"If there is a God, I don't understand how he does some of the terrible things he does."

"Again you are right. As Saint Augustine said, the understood God is no God. You want things to make sense. The only way to have that is to believe in a God beyond your understanding."

"That's too cute for me. I won't to go there."

"You're a hard man to please. You won't accept advanced science, you won't accept random luck, you insist that things make sense, but you won't accept God. There's only one thing left, and that is to make up your own ideas about why things happen."

"I can't just make it up. I want to handle the reality."

"Absolutely! There is the reality that evil things happen in the world. That's absolutely real. And so do you want to have a way of understanding what causes that evil? You can use any word you want for the cause of evil. The popular one is the devil. It seems clear that you believe in the devil. Believing in the devil is another way of saying 'I know there is evil in the world'. And a police chief whose job it is to deal with murder, surely knows, as well as he knows anything, that evil exists."

"I don't believe in the devil."

"We just demonstrated that you do. You just don't like the word. You can pick any other word you want. But unless you use the word devil, no one will understand you."

"I can't go there."

"But that's where you have to go to expand your mind to include all of reality. That is where you have to go to understand your case and do the best you can."

Mercedes was sitting in her office when the door opened without any notice. "Maria? What is it?"

"Dave is in the hospital. He tried to kill himself."

"No."

"Yes. He shot himself in the head late last night.

"Why?"

"He left a note." She handed it to Mercedes.

> *To my beloved Maria, and all who care for me.*
> *I know that I am a sinner and this is my greatest sin.*
> *I know that my Lord Jesus Christ forbids me to do this,*
> *but my soul prays for His forgiveness. I know that I did*
> *not kill them. I did not. And since I am not responsible*
> *for their deaths, I should not feel guilty. But I feel the*
> *guilt. I know we are taught that we are all sinners, and*
> *all guilty, but this guilt is different. When I came back*
> *from the service, my life was destroyed. But with the love*
> *of Maria and Jesus, my life was rebuilt. The church is*

the blood in my body. The church is the air that I
breathe. The church was my life. Forgive me, Maria.

Mercedes sank to her chair sobbing. "Oh, Maria, is there anything I can do?"

"No, I need all my strength now not to follow him."

"Is he dead?"

"No, he's in the intensive care unit. They took him to surgery last night, and the doctor said there is hope."

"When you go to the hospital, can I come with you?"

"If you want to, yes. That would be very sweet." Later that day, Mercedes told Linda what happened. Linda said she felt indebted to Dave for helping her get to Mexico. She asked to come to the hospital also, and Maria approved. That evening, all three women were in his hospital room, on their knees, praying for his recovery.

CHAPTER 40

I must say something

It had been a long, hard day for the mayor. The phone had not stopped ringing. Senators, actually calling themselves, not just their assistants. The same with the governor, the press, and a variety of important people that he could not ignore. It had been a long, hard day. The mayor leaned back in his chair and closed his eyes.

What do they want from me? El Sueño is unreachable in Mexico and says he did it under orders of the mysterious queen, the force, God knows what. ...

He must have given Linda some drugs for her to believe this crap. ... She's a damn good looker. She's not stupid, but how could she repeat this fairytale? Mercedes said she was hot for him. Maybe it's a love interest trying to cover up.

Maybe he's tied into the Russian oligarch's narco friends. That doesn't explain how Agri got those people to testify that they knew the queen. And those were high-level people. They couldn't be bought, and they don't work together. The queen idea - impossible to swallow and now it has become impossible to spit out. I don't know. I don't know. I don't know. ... I just want it all to go away.

They don't have to get elected. I'm to go out and sell this craziness to the public and the big shots who keep calling me? It won't work. I'll be a laughingstock. There's no way I can do that.

The alternative to 'the queen' is to sell to the public the idea that Alteman was killed by a devil. They think I can do it without getting run out of town. Holy shit! Not only is the 'idea' crazy but 'they' are crazy to think I can get away with it. I guess the super religious like that cop's wife will go for that, but no one else. They keep saying there simply is no other alternative. Well not exactly ... he wasn't killed by a devil, but the murder was organized and directed by a devil. All of the separate things that were done as part of the plot to murder him were done by ordinary people. ... I should go home and go to sleep. They're used to the idea of the devil manipulating people.

Mercedes got that fancy professor. He seems a nice guy, but no one's gonna take that philosophy stuff. If I try to tell people that I believe this murder was the result of mysterious forces that no one could understand.

I have to say something. The case has gone on for so long. I'm tired of this crap. I should go into a different business.

I haven't the foggiest idea what to say. But I have to say something. I guess I could say simply that the case is not yet solved. The trouble with that is that it doesn't do me any good. They will be back the next day asking again. And every time they ask, I look stupid. You don't get elected looking stupid. ...

It might be a good idea to blame the investigation. Say the police did a bad job. Say, I'm going to clean house and bring in fresh competent people.... I don't think I can sell it and the truth is they did a pretty good job. It's just a weird case. ... I just want it all to go away.

We could charge Agri. His fingerprints are on the case with sending the money. Even the money to buy the gun. He's a slimy bastard. He deserves to go to prison. He might even be guilty. He certainly is guilty of aiding and abetting the crime. But it does look a little bit stupid to convict him of that when I can't say who, or what he was helping. But I'm pretty sure he's not guilty ... really. There's no way he could get the cowgirl to set Alteman up. That's the other problem. He'll fight the case and he might win. That way we will look stupid. ...

We could blame Gulov. At least he's dead and can't argue about it. And the public will believe anything about a Russian oligarch. And the truth is he had a motive. And he was friends with the narco big boys. And it might be true. They kill somebody almost every day and more than one on Sundays. It's a good fit. But it's not that kind of murder. They just get one of their boys with a machine gun to put 47 holes all over his body.

I can sell it, but I can't believe it. My friends will say I'm a hypocrite to say one thing and believe another. It's unfortunate hypocrisy has such a bad name. It's really rather important. It's the essential grease of life that allows one to fit the square peg of principle into the round hole of reality. Gulov is the best idea yet. ... I should go home and go to sleep.

I can't blame it on God. The public only knows the good side of Alteman. Even if they would accept that God arranges the death of bad people, they would never accept it for a good man. I guess I could publicize his bad side. That might work. It's risky when the good side comes out. The same with the devil. If the devil killed him because he was too good, what do we do with the bad side? Most of the good side is old. I could say he changed. I could say his success ruined him. I can sell that. It might be better than blaming Gulov.

That brings it back to this 'queen' craziness. There's no way to sell that. The real trouble is they almost have me believing it. It's better not to call it a queen. It's better to call it luck, or coincidence, or I don't know what. But you can't stand up in front of the public and call it seriously the queen or any shit like that.

If there was just one part to the murder plot, I could sell luck or coincidence, but with so many separate pieces, and a lot of that is already known to the public, there's no way. .... beats the shit out of me. Whatever I have to sell, I don't know what to believe myself. It's just crazy.

The docs have a saying, 'First, do no harm'. Gulov is dead. Nothing I say will harm him.

CHAPTER 41

THAT ENDS WELL

"I am going to Chiapas."

"Say that again?"

"You heard me correctly. I'm going to Chiapas."

"Just for the scenery?"

"No, to meet Pablito."

"And just how are you going to do that?"

"The same way you did. I put an ad in the newspaper, and they answered. It's a secret. You can't tell anyone."

"You have another case?"

"No. I want to meet him. He sounds more interesting than any of the other men I've met."

"Are you crazy? Don't do it!"

"You don't want to share him? Do you want him for yourself?"

"No." After a long pause, "I have children here. And I still harbor dreams of getting Tyrone back. Pablito is out of the question for me. But I see your point. I see your point. In another life, I might do it too."

The mayor stood in front of a large crowd of reporters. "I know that all of you have been interested in who murdered Mr. Theodore Alteman. Mr. Alteman was a distinguished American, and his murder shocked all of us. He had made several major contributions both to the country and to many individuals. I had met Ted more than a few times, and I can say he was one of the most remarkable people I've ever met. It is amazing that for many of the individuals whom he helped, often when they were in the most destitute circumstances, he did so anonymously. They did not even know his name until they saw his picture in the paper.

After he was murdered, the police have worked tirelessly on this case. The police have interviewed dozens and dozens of people who have been touched by this case, including not just people who were close to Ted and who are affected by his death, but dozens more who may have had some role in his death. One of our officers has traveled to New York, Las Vegas, and Monterey Mexico, to interview people who just might help us. Although the police have done great work, we cannot make an arrest at this time. We will be lowering the intensity of the investigation, in part because we think we understand how the murder occurred, and we have a pretty good idea as to who ordered it.

As you know, Ted had won a number of amazing court cases for huge sums of money. Those who lost those cases did not appreciate Ted's virtues. The plot to murder him was very complicated and organized with great resources. Again, we cannot make an arrest at this time, but we feel sure we have a good idea who did it and why. The public can be confident that we will not rest until we bring the murderers to justice.

Some of you may remember one of Ted's greatest triumphs, his court victory for an unbelievable sum of money against the dark forces that infect our society with tentacles even to Hollywood. These dark forces are spread all over the world from Russian oligarchs to Latin American narco-traffickers, to our own mafia and other criminals. We believe that they are behind this. We don't know how they did it and we don't know through whom they did it. But we are convinced that it was done by that kind of dark force.

The public can be confident that we will not rest until we bring the murderers to justice.

For now, let us mourn the death of this good man, and remember his contribution to our country."

Tyrone stepped into the mayor's office and sat down. The mayor paused for a long moment and made strong eye contact with Tyrone. He braced himself for the task and prided himself that he would try to bring some good out of this mess. "What you just heard me say to the press is part of my role as a working politician. Sometimes, without lying, we have to say things that don't quite mean what they appear. But you have a unique situation in the story, and I want to tell you what I really believe. What I want to explain to you, Mr. Neal would have been to me so unbelievable as to have been crazy even a few weeks ago, before I knew what I know now, but on my word of honor, every word is true. First of all, the murder of Theodore Alteman is now closed. Our understanding of how and why he died comes from the heroic work of your ex-wife. She allowed herself to be kidnapped by murderers, in order to learn the truth."

"I know. They asked me to do it, and I refused."

"She then convinced them to let her return to us with that knowledge. She is a hero. The murder of Mr. Alteman was done in a way that is not humanly possible. That is the most amazing fact in the case. It was done with the use of power that no human being possesses. As I said, until a few weeks ago, I would have said such a statement is ridiculous, but now I know that it's true."

"What does that mean?"

"We all know that there are events in life which we cannot explain. We all need to humble ourselves before that truth. It has not been easy for me. Some of us are lucky enough to get that humility by the grace of God. I cannot say that for myself. Some of us ascribe it to either good or bad luck, as the case may be, or some other random process. There's nothing wrong with that. But now I believe, as I never did before, that there are forces acting in the world that have their own reasons, good and bad, for which we are simply the playthings of their whims. Ted Alteman had a long-standing relationship with those forces. For many years, they made him one of the most remarkable and successful men in this country, and in the world generally. But as time went along, he became more arrogant and independent of the direction he received from those who gave him those powers. In the end, they came to recognize the evil he was doing, and they had him murdered. From what I have learned since then, he deserved it."

Tyrone exhaled and slumped. "I'm not inclined to accept the idea of mysterious powers. Let me tell it to you straight, sir. I had a belly full of religious mumbo-jumbo when I was a kid before I even went to college. The preacher in our church was banging my 15-year-old sister even while my parents thought he was the most wonderful person. Don't try to sell me any of that crap. I am not religious, even one iota."

"Neither am I. You know Mr. Neal, we have more in common than you might know. I also come from the mountains back east. We're good stock. Honestly, we built this country. We are ready to stand up and fight for what we believe in. That's why I was in the Marines. Ted's brother is a Marine and I knew him slightly when I was in the service. And when the going gets tough, we hold on, dig in, and continue to fight. Before I went into politics, I was a cop. Cops get a lot wrong, but I liked the police business because I know we are always fighting on the right side. But sometimes, not often, but sometimes, we have to let go. We have to accept that there are things we can't change, we can't do, and we can't even sometimes get even."

"Where does that leave me?"

"Ted was once a very good man. But as time went on the success, the power, corrupted him. One of his many later failings, which I think those powers recognized, and for which he received that just punishment, was the seduction of your wife. He used the powers that they had given him to manipulate your wife's behavior. She, or any human being, would have struggled in the face of that power. The believers would say Mr. Alteman had become an agent of the devil. As they would have said, in the past, truthfully, and now we have to learn how to say it again, your wife was, at a minimum, thrown off balance by influences beyond her. I don't think her real inner self is responsible for being unfaithful to you."

"Do you want me to accept that? You want me to think of her as a victim?"

"Yes, sir. I do I think it's the truth."

"That's one hell of a long stretch. She tore the heart out of me and then stepped on it. You have no idea how much I have hated her."

"I'm sure you're right. I haven't lived in your shoes, so I have no intention of telling you how to understand your life. But I am a man, a husband, and a politician. I have dealt with a lot of different people in a lot of different situations. I can empathize with your pain. But as a politician I know, and as a very successful lawyer you know, sometimes things are not simple. You have my word of honor, this matter is not simple. Mercedes and the other people who have worked with you on this case tell me that, even after all the pain and all the hate, you love her. My advice to you as a man is to go with the love."

Tyrone burst into tears. "Thank you."

"Don't thank me. I did nothing. Everything was done by your wife and Captain Herrera."

"What about the police officer who worked on the case, Dave Good? I heard that he shot himself."

"He did. He was a member of the church where there was the massacre. He blamed himself. But he got lucky. His hand must've been shaking when he pulled the trigger. I'm told he's making a remarkable recovery."

"Where is Captain Mercedes so I can thank her?"

"She has resigned from the police force, emptied her apartment, and no one we know has seen her for over a week."

"Is she OK?"

"We don't know. That's the end of the story."

Linda stepped out from behind the partition. She looked at Tyrone with tears in her eyes, and he looked back with similar tears. After a long pause, she got down on her knees and started to walk on her knees toward him. Looking up at him she said, "Can you forgive me?"

He reached down to help her to stand up. They kissed. "Yes, with all my heart and soul."

THE END